The Lieutenant's Lady

The
Lieutenant's
Lady

By BESS STREETER ALDRICH

University of Nebraska Press
Lincoln and London

First Bison Book printing: 1987
Most recent printing indicated by the first digit below:
1   2   3   4   5   6   7   8   9   10

Library of Congress Cataloging-in-Publication Data
Aldrich, Bess Streeter, 1881–1954.
   The lieutenant's lady.
   "Bison book."
   I. Title.
[PS3501.L378L5   1987]   813'.52   87-4994
ISBN 0-8032-5914-X (pbk.)

Reprinted by arrangement with E. P. Dutton, a division of
New American Library

The names of all characters in this book are purely fictitious. If the
name of any living person is used it is simply a coincidence.

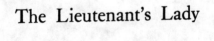

The Lieutenant's Lady

Chapter I

SEVENTY-FIVE years ago a young woman kept a diary in which she wrote some of her innermost thoughts, many of the daily happenings, and all of the weather.

This story is a fictionized version of that real diary. The thoughts more or less trite and pedantic have been curtailed, the happenings (for obvious reasons) sometimes changed, but the weather remains practically intact.

She was a modern girl of those late eighteen-sixties—our leading lady—for in her mushroom skirts, her silk manteau and butter-bowl hat, she set her face toward an adventure which led to exciting events and emotional experiences.

So, step out of the yellowed diary, Linnie Colsworth, and let us see your smooth dark hair, wide brown eyes, and warm generous mouth. Recreate yourself from the fading ink of its pages and help us understand something of the stanch heart that beat under those hard little stays, bidding you defy convention three-quarters of a century ago.

As the diary begins, so begins the story.

It is in the territory of Nebraska. *Ne-brath-ke*—in the Otoe Indian language, "flat water." In the town of *O-ma-ha,* meaning "above all others on a stream." Omaha! Now a city of homes, churches, and colleges, factories, airports, and bomber plants. Then but a raw new town above all others on a stream in the land of flat water.

An orator of the day said the young city stood there on the Missouri River like a goddess lighting the way to the territory's hospitable borders and to the great west beyond. A disgruntled investor said the town wallowed in the mud like a harlot plucking at travelers' sleeves and begging them to stay with her.

Whatever the interpretation of it, Omaha sprawled over the Missouri flats and the river bluffs, muddy or dusty, sun-browned or snow-packed, but always lustily noisy with the vehemence of youth and growth.

The war between the states was over, and hordes of land seekers poured into the west. Their canvas-covered wagons, stocked with supplies for the long trek, stood in the streets and in vacant acreages of the rambling town.

But not all new-comers were seeking homes beyond the little city perched there on the river's bank. Farnam and Douglas streets already boasted many brick buildings, while up and down these two principal thoroughfares were a dozen yawning excavations, like the cavities of missing teeth in some giant denture, into which new ones were to be fitted. Even the side streets held a few scattered stores.

Up on a high hill stood the white territorial capitol (reportedly with a bar in the basement for the convenience of arid legislators), although it was soon to be removed out on the prairie, to the infinite disgust of Omahans and the scattered settlers north of the Platte River.

Already the young town had begun to put on airs by denying the privilege of stacking hay in the streets and passing an ordinance that any hogs found running loose were to be impounded and sold.

Freighters, land speculators, soldiers, blanketed Indians, transient railroad workers mingled in the streets with the permanent settlers. Dressed in eastern styles, the wives and daughters of the leading citizenry picked their way daintily through slush, mud, or dust, while at their elbows calico-clad women in sunbonnets went in and out of the stores, all alike discreetly averting their eyes when the orange-haired "other kind" went by.

Every morning stage-coaches, bulging with passengers, left for Topeka, Kansas, or Denver in the Colorado Territory, or back to Denison, Iowa, to meet at its terminus the incoming train from the east. Every day the steam ferry-boat crossed and recrossed the Missouri, plying between Omaha and the older Council Bluffs where Abe Lincoln had stood on a high cliff only a few years before and surveyed the distant territory, saying, "Not one but many railroads will center here."

Although the first sixty miles of the Union Pacific

to North Bend had been laid, no train smoke yet polluted the rolling country. Only the steamboats coming up from St. Louis sent their billowing smoke and
their hoarse whistling into the prairie air.

The majority of Omaha houses were modest when
not downright crude log cabins and tar-paper shacks,
but a half-dozen really fine ones sat proudly behind
their picket fences. Some were of brick, some of
lumber, both commodities being equally high-priced
and scarce. A priority then meaning merely "first
come, first served," Henry L. Colsworth, the possessor of one of the nicest of these homes, had a way
of seeing to it that he always had a priority.

There had been much speculation about the possibility of the Union Pacific starting from the older
Bellevue, a few miles down the river, and a few
poor guessers, practically giving away their Omaha
lots, had purchased property there on the chance
that it would become the Nebraska terminus. But
Henry L. Colsworth had gambled on Omaha, and
Omaha had won. So now, for every hundred dollars
he had brought with him to the new west, he possessed several thousand.

The Colsworth house stood behind its white picket
fence on a corner which one day would be in the
center of solid business blocks but which in the late
sixties was merely a good location for a nice home
with its barn, carriage house, cow-shed, pig-pen and
grassy yard.

The house itself had a New England look, as

though it might have been transported bodily from Concord or Lexington, an upright and long wing with wide white-painted weather boarding and generous green blinds. And the inside bore out the exterior's promise. The shining new parlor was rather magnificent for anything in the territory: a fine flowered carpet, heavy mahogany furniture, dark tasseled drapes, Nottingham lace curtains, one of the new Rogers groups, pictures of nosegays in oval frames, steel cuts of famous historical events, a sturdy square piano brought up from St. Louis by boat, and, as the last touch in exquisite taste, a bust of Mozart looking down in supercilious silence on any potential performer.

Here to-night in this sumptuous new parlor was Linnie Colsworth, recently arrived from the east to stay with her Uncle Henry Colsworth, Aunt Louise, and Cousin Cynthia for a whole year. A journey was a journey in the sixties, and when one finally arrived at its wearisome end one was prone to settle down for a time.

As the plan stood now she was to remain here until the following spring, then go up the Missouri River by steamboat to the (likewise new) Iowa town of Sioux City, in order to spend a few weeks with a seminary friend who had married and come west. From there she could take the stage to the western terminus of the Illinois Central—the railroad might even be finished into Sioux City by that time—and back to New York.

So here she was for a long visit and already a co-hostess at her first western social event, a party to which Cousin Cynthia had invited a dozen young people.

There was Cynthia, herself, fair-haired, vivacious, as fluttery as a night moth and almost as irresponsible. There were five other Omaha young ladies dressed in their voluminous best gowns, a little palpitant at the proximity of so much masculinity. There were six young men of the professional type. One, a George Hemming, dry-goods clerk, was apparently the town cut-up, as the girls all started to laugh before he was fairly launched on any of his almost continuous remarks. And there was Lieutenant Norman Stafford, an officer in the Regular Army, who was in Omaha on leave while en route to Fort Leavenworth, Kansas.

The Regular Army, but lately finished with its war work, was now being called upon to relieve state troops in the west where, farther out on the prairie, the Sioux and Cheyennes were destroying cabins and wagon trains. Indeed, the Indians were so troublesome that some of the eastern insurance policies of the day contained a pointed paragraph to the effect that benefits accruing were null and void in case you crossed the Missouri River and were massacred.

But all that possible carnage was remote from the pleasant party to-night.

No young man had arrived with a girl, but all

would squire the ladies home. Two fathers and a brother had brought their daughters and sister in buggies through the mud just as dusk was falling, depositing them at the new carriage block, thankful their duties were over. A pair of twin sisters had picked their own way down the moist hilly street, juggling from hand to hand the bags containing their best shoes, while trying to hold their identical dresses and long fringed shawls from the spring rivulets.

So far the party had consisted of much polite conversation, charades, and dancing. But now George Hemming, the cut-up, was asking Cynthia to play and sing.

After a satisfactory period of coaxing from the guests and demure reluctance from Cynthia, there she was at the piano beginning a ballad.

Several of the others grouped themselves around her. Lieutenant Stafford sauntered to the back of the instrument to stand in the shadows where he could drink in her fair loveliness.

A man whose name was Johnny Sands had married Betty Hague
And though she brought him gold and lands she proved a terrible plague.

So while Cynthia is leading in the lively and lengthy ballad, with some of the others joining in heartily, there is time to dip back into the past a bit.

The two Colsworth cousins were daughters of

brothers. Linnie's parents had died when she was small, and she had lived since with maternal relatives in the Washington Square district of New York, so that only as a little girl had she held any association with the Henry Colsworth family. But when Uncle Henry, accompanied by Cynthia, had come east on business, he had looked her up and insisted that she return with them for a long visit. He had been anxious to get back home but had allowed Cynthia to stay a while and take in the New York sights when he found she would have Linnie's company on the long trip to Omaha.

All the way out from the east, Linnie had listened to Cynthia singing the praises of this Lieutenant Stafford whom she had met at a party given for the army officers stationed on Governor's Island.

Cynthia had voiced her laudations until Linnie was tired hearing about the paragon—on the cinder-filled cars to Chicago, off and on during the twelve-hour wait there when they missed the western train, occasionally on the tedious ride out to Denison, Iowa, surreptitiously on the crowded stage from Denison to Council Bluffs, even a lingering bit on the ferry crossing to Omaha.

That stage ride had been the most disagreeable part of the long journey, miring down in the mud the last six miles, and so crowded, with all the other passengers men: an officer for Fort Laramie, a young doctor talking about getting up his shingle in Denver, drummers to sell goods in the river towns.

At the many half-concealed but admiring glances cast toward the girls, Cynthia would whisper, "Oh, I don't know what I'd have done without you, Linnie. I'd have been too scared with all these men."

But Linnie knew better. The one thing Cynthia would never be afraid of was men.

Over and over Cynthia had talked of her lieutenant friend's charms. He was to be transferred to Fort Leavenworth, Kansas, but he was going to ask for leave to come to Omaha first and take a boat down the river to the fort.

"I'll just admire to have you see him, Linnie. He's my ideal . . . right out of a novel. And I know he intends to ask me for my hand when he comes."

And then to Linnie's wondering surprise, after all the glorification of the lieutenant, when they were on the ferry crossing the Missouri, with the white territorial capitol of home in plain sight, Cynthia had suddenly begun to remember a young man in Omaha —George Hemming.

"I'll admire to have you know him, Linnie. He's so full of hi-jinks . . . he just keeps you in stitches."

It had all turned out as Cynthia wished. *She's one of those kittenish girls who always have their own way,* Linnie was saying to herself. For Lieutenant Norman Stafford had succeeded in getting permission to come by the way of Omaha, and here he was standing back of the piano, not singing like the others but scarcely able to take his eyes from Cynthia's pale prettiness.

And for once, Cynthia, the fly-up-the-creek, was right. He *was* fine and strangely attractive, with his lean strong face and well-knit uniformed figure.

And there was the George Hemming whom Cynthia had talked about, too, looking plump and sleek, singing clowningly, full of his capers, making Cynthia the center of his attention.

Standing back a little herself, Linnie was thinking how easily Cynthia did everything. Even her piano playing was characteristic of her, not at all accurate but made to appear so. Part of the time she could even look up from the keys at the young men around her, roll her eyes, and drop them coyly when their answering looks held her.

I can't be coy, Linnie was thinking. *I'm just not made to be flirtatious. I only know how to be cordial or cold . . . friendly or unfriendly. I don't seem to know any of the little between ways.*

Cynthia had changed to another song now, the sad legend of the Weeping Water:

> *Oh do you remember the Indian tale*
> *Of the maidens who wept by the creek in the vale*
> *For the braves who were slain in Nehawka?*

She was looking soulfully at the lieutenant and then smilingly at George Hemming.

It rather embarrassed Linnie to have Cynthia singling out the two for her coquetry, and before every one.

And the little creek fed by their weeping all day
Rose into a river that wended its way
To the sea with the tears from Nehawka.

She found herself wondering what the lieutenant would think of Cynthia if he knew how self-centered she was underneath those dainty soft ways. But a man in love never saw through that kind. He was just too fine to be hoodwinked by some one who would twist him around her little finger. Then she began to question how she knew he was so fine. An army man that way—maybe he was horrid—probably he wasn't anywhere near good enough for Cynthia. No, that wasn't true. What made her think so? She just knew. There was something about that grave manner, that lean sunburned face, those steady gray eyes.

But here was Olga, the Swedish woman who came across the alley every day to help with the housework, making pantomimic motions from the double doors of the back parlor to signal that refreshments were ready.

Long before this time, already after half-past ten, Aunt Louise, a delicate little wisp of a person, had succumbed to the excitement and gone up to bed. So Cynthia passed the candy hearts with their red mottoes, and there was much laughter over the matching of them for partners to walk into the dining-room.

And then Linnie found herself with the identical motto of Cynthia's lieutenant—*I saw you wink—*

and for some reason or other was strangely excited over the trivial happening.

The seven couples marched through the back parlor and into the fine dark-paneled dining-room, with George Hemming in the lead calling back that they looked as though they were going into the ark two by two, and—swinging one arm back and forth slowly from his face like a trunk—that he and Cynthia were the elephants.

"Our friend George," the lieutenant said low to Linnie, "he's quite a card, isn't he?"

"The joker," she whispered back. And they both laughed.

She liked the way his grave eyes crinkled suddenly and the corners of his mouth drew downward in their droll grin.

But all the others were laughing by that time, too, for Aunt Louise's parrot, excited over the crowd coming in, was thumping her scabby old legs up and down on the floor of her cage and calling raucously: "Ha! Ha! Fit to kill."

The mahogany sideboard was crowded with dishes of food which Olga soon passed to the guests sitting in chairs around the wall. There were platters of cold chicken and sliced beef and pork, buttered raised biscuits and pickles and jam, and two silver baskets piled high with huge wedges of cake.

Sometimes Olga in her friendly way would urge: "Oh, take more'n dat. I got blenty in kitchen."

While eating was the prime occupation, there was

much low talk between partners, but when it grew too quiet Polly would emit sadly the one other phrase in her repertoire: "So sorry! So sorry!"

Linnie could not remember when she had enjoyed a person more than her partner. Sometimes young men were shy when they talked to her, and, feeling sorry for them, she would carry the burden of the conversation. Sometimes they were silly, trying to please her with bungling compliments, so that she had only dislike for them.

But this Lieutenant Stafford was neither one. He was sensible and interesting, treating her as though she were an intelligent person and not a flirt or a dolt.

They talked about the east and the places there they knew in common. Sometimes she asked him questions about army life to which he gave thoughtful answers. Once when he looked across at her cousin in that fascinated way she had noticed before, she said, to test him: "Cynthia's pretty, isn't she?"

"She's . . . everything," he answered tensely.

This was no polite surface talk but sincere and serious. It made her envy Cynthia a little, wondering if she could comprehend his feeling, was mature enough to meet it in kind. Then she smiled ironically —talking that way to herself, as though she were years older than Cynthia instead of five months.

Suddenly there was commotion in the kitchen, a great stomping of feet and bellowing of voice. The dining-room door swung back, and no longer did the party belong to the young people. For Uncle Henry had arrived.

He was a large man. Vitality exuded from every pore. His two-part whiskers were long and flowing, his vest expansive but seemingly held down by the huge gold links of a watch-chain and cigar-cutter.

Although it inconvenienced every one with his plate, Uncle Henry shook hands all around, chucked the girls under their chins and told them they were as pretty as pansies. He asked the young men what they were doing these days to make Omaha known to the easterners and sometimes insisted embarrassingly on finding out whether they were Union-Republicans or Democrats, dropping their hands as though they were hot coals if they ventured to acknowledge the latter. It was as though a midwestern tornado had struck the house, with Polly adding her screeching, "Ha! Ha! Fit to kill."

Finally Uncle Henry withdrew, and it was like the passing of the storm.

Refreshments over and with Polly stumping about in agitation at their leaving, the crowd all went into the parlor to end the evening singing again, this time on a sentimental how-can-I-bear-to-leave-thee note.

The party was breaking up, the men asking the young ladies if they might have the pleasure of their company home. Because it was moonlight there were no lanterns out on the porch, although George Hemming said audaciously that he always kept one in his buggy so young ladies' parents would trust him.

Every one came up to Linnie to bid her good night, some of the young men saying politely: "I'm sorry you don't have to be escorted anywhere." But of them all, the one who attracted her had eyes only for Cynthia.

The crowd was at the door, then out on the porch, with many formal speeches for the pleasant evening, and only Lieutenant Norman Stafford was left, standing near the piano examining the song-books there.

Linnie knew he was remaining to be with Cynthia alone, so she slipped out to the back stairway and up to the room the girls shared. There she lighted her lamp and looked in the oval glass over the highboy, studying her appearance, comparing it with Cynthia's. Dark smooth hair where Cynthia's was light and fluffy. Serious dark eyes. Cynthia's were blue and childlike. Wide mouth. Cynthia's was a red embroidered buttonhole.

"Just plain and ladylike and uninteresting," she said disparagingly to the reflection there. "Sort of a female calf."

She turned away from her youthful image with distaste and undressed for bed.

After a long time she heard the soft rustle of Cynthia's skirts on the stairway, caught a whiff of *eau de cologne,* and sensed that her cousin was tiptoeing in.

"Linnie!" The scent was stronger. "Are you awake?"

She jumped with assumed confusion and sat up. "Oh . . . you startled me."

Cynthia put her lamp on the highboy and climbed up on the edge of the bed, settling herself in a swirling nest of blue.

"Well, Linnie . . . look at me. I'm betrothed."

"George? Or the lieutenant?"

"Oh, Linnie, how funny you are." Cynthia laughed, but softly so as not to waken her parents. "Mrs. Norman Stafford, wife of Lieutenant Stafford, an officer in the Regular Army. How does that sound?"

"It sounds . . . very nice. So it's the lieutenant?"

"Norman! I call him Norman now, and you can, too, because he will be your cousin. You like him, don't you, Linnie?"

"Why, yes . . . I like him . . . very much."

A bit of the girl's amiability fell away. "But not *too* much. Don't think I didn't see you at refreshment time. You know he's mine."

Sitting there with arms around her knees, her dark hair pleated in neat braids, Linnie was suddenly remembering from a little-girl past: "You can't have that doll either, Linnie. They're all mine."

But she only said, "I'm glad for you . . . and I hope you'll be happy, Cynthia. What are your plans?"

"Well, first he has to go to that old Fort Leavenworth, but maybe he'll be sent back to Governor's Island, and I could live in New York then. Or he might be sent to Washington. I would just admire to be in Washington society. They say the army crowd is having parties..."

"But, Cynthia, when you marry him you'll be an army wife. You'll have to go anywhere he's ordered. It might be farther out west to that Fort Laramie or up the river to those Dakota Territory forts your father was telling us about or..."

"Oh, he wouldn't be sent there...not as handsome and citified an officer as *he* is." She pursed her small mouth a moment, then changed to low laughter. "Linnie, you should have seen George. It was too funny. He was trying to be the last one to leave, and he hung back and hung back, but Norman just went over to the piano and started looking at the music so unconcerned, and I said, 'George, would you be so kind as to accompany Victoria and Virgilla to their home?' And there was nothing he could say but 'With pleasure,' and go with them. You should have seen the look he gave me when he left ...cross with me, but melting, too, and so sad. Oh, my good granny!"

She put her hands to her face in chuckling remembrance, then dropped them to say excitedly: "I gave him my picture—the tinted one in the white carved case, and he is going to send me one of him."

"George?"

"No, silly! *Norman!*" She smiled to herself again with memory of the evening. "Do you know, Linnie, I'm going to feel downright sorry for him, thinking so much of me the way I just know he does."

"The lieutenant?"

"No, *Geor*.... Oh, you go on, you tease!"

After Cynthia had come to bed, Linnie lay and looked out toward the river. A long time afterward, when sleep had not come, she rose quietly and went over to the window. Life was so queer. Here she was thinking about Norman Stafford, who was over at the Hernden House thinking about Cynthia, who had been chattering away about George Hemming.

The May moon shone down on the river and the levee and the steamboats tied there. She could hear all the night sounds of the sprawling town—cattle bawling, the throbbing of a steamer's engine, ribald laughter, the pounding on some building where they were working by the light of the moon, a near-by "Gee ... gee" (did those freighters never sleep?), almost the slosh-slosh of the muddy river against the piling of the dock.

To-morrow morning that same river would carry him away. But what difference would that make? He was away already. He was Cynthia's. *And the little creek fed by their weeping all day ... rose into a river that wended its way ... to the sea with the tears from Nehawka.*

Chapter II

LINNIE went down to breakfast, tired from her half-sleepless night and cross with herself because it had been so. Envying another girl her young man was bad enough at any time, but when the girl was your own cousin and you scarcely existed in the man's sight, it took on the quality of being addled in the head.

Cynthia, however, was gay and talkative because of her new happiness, the whole breakfast centering around the subject of her betrothal.

At least she attempted to have it center around herself, for it was never possible that any human could be the middle point in a circle if Henry Colsworth were near.

Aunt Louise was at the table, too, this morning. One never knew whether or not she would appear. She was enjoying delicate health, which rather set her apart from the feminine portion of a town whose pioneer women largely were hale and sturdy.

When one of Aunt Louise's weak spells overtook her, she accepted it passively. At the least physical excitement or the slightest exercising of an emotion she would say resignedly, "It's come," and get comfortably into bed. Her blue-veined face looked like a piece of delicate Chelsea ware. Her pale hair was parted and combed tightly down to a heavy bun at the nape of her slight neck, which gave her ears, unusually large for so small a person, an appearance of standing out nakedly as handles do on a china vase. Gentle and colorless, she seconded her breezy husband's decisive statements like a faint and hesitant echo.

Just now, after the excitement of her daughter's betrothal, it was all she could do to hold up her head through the long meal. There were boiled potatoes and dried codfish gravy, oatmeal and cream and hot corn bread, and Uncle Henry was attacking them all with gusto even as he talked.

"The young man spoke to me privately in New York, and I took pains to inquire about everything. When I found out the well-to-do York state family he came from ... then I said to myself I knew...." Yes, Uncle Henry was assuming much of the conversation and all of the credit. "I like the young man but I don't like the army connection. We'll have to see about him locating here. All kinds of opportunities to get ahead. But he'll never get anywhere in the army. I can put him on to something suitable."

"Yes, Cynthia, we can get him something suitable," Aunt Louise echoed, like the daughter of Air and Earth who pined away until nothing was left but her voice.

It occurred to Linnie over her corn bread that Norman Stafford did not seem like a young man who could be pushed around into something suitable.

"He told me he felt quite devoted to the army," she volunteered.

Cynthia bristled. "I guess *I'm* the one who knows about *that*."

"Oh, well, the army's work will all be over in a few years anyway." Uncle Henry disposed of the future of the United States Army with one sweeping sentence and a wave of the hand. "The dirty Injuns'll all be cleaned up and there'll be nothing more for the army to do. Towns are growing up around the forts now. Look how Fort Des Moines came along, and Fort Dodge, Fort Madison, Fort Wayne, and all the others... and now Fort Leavenworth, Fort Scott, Fort Collins, and dozens of 'em will come along the same way."

If only all the disturbing events of the early days of the trans-Missouri country could have been settled as easily and decisively as Henry Colsworth was settling them verbally!

"Now that the war's over, the next thing is to lick the hide off the Injuns... and then there'll be peace for two hundred years."

"Ha! Ha! Fit to kill," Polly called out from her cage.

Olga came in with fresh corn bread, talked readily about the news of the betrothal, too much a friend and neighbor of the family to be called a hired girl.

"I got two pattern new qvilts, Cynthy, de *evenin'
star* and one dey say to me is *floo de liss.*"

"They don't have that kind in the army, Olga,"
Linnie laughed. "Just army blankets."

"You seem to think you know a lot about it."
Cynthia's voice had a sharp edge.

Uncle Henry told Olga to speak to Magnus about
getting the horses hitched. Magnus was Olga's husband, and although there was scarcely enough for
him to do around the place all day it pleased Uncle
Henry to have a stableman and to be driven the few
blocks to his office behind a pair of spanking bays.

The shingle in front of that second-story office
said "Lawyer," but inasmuch as there were fifty-
five of the species in the young town, it was merely
a title behind which to carry on multiple activities,
buying and selling real estate, speculating in various
commodities, constructing a new store building or
two to rent, and, although he was not a member of
the territorial legislature, doing a great deal of
"fixing" in back rooms behind closed doors.

So Uncle Henry went to his office, and Aunt
Louise, tired from her struggle with a boiled potato,
lay down on the horsehair sofa. Olga trudged in and
out carrying away the dishes. Cynthia, in a pink print
which made her look like a grown-up doll, dusted
Mozart in the parlor and a black-framed picture of
Lincoln in the back parlor. And Linnie, no longer
mere company, went upstairs to make beds.

Some time later when she came down, Norman Stafford was there in the parlor saying good-by to Cynthia. Seeing her, the two came out into the hall, so that Linnie shook hands with him and said good-by, too.

He looked very fresh and fine this morning in his uniform.

For a moment he stood looking gravely down at Linnie, crisp and pretty in her blue-and-white striped print. "I want to thank you for our pleasant conversation last evening. I found you most intelligent."

She flushed to the roots of her hair and said: "I thank you heartily." Both procedures were characteristic of the day.

"You'll look after her, Miss Linnie?" His gray eyes, warm with their new love, were on Cynthia. "This is the first time 'the girl I left behind me' ever meant anything to me but a noisy tune." Then he turned back to Linnie, and the corners of his mouth drew down in their droll way: "And keep your left eye on that funny-man, George, too."

It was as though they alone knew a secret, laughing together that way.

Linnie said indeed she would, with Cynthia pouting coyly: "Oh, you two! You're just trying to make out I'm flirtatious!"

Then Linnie went upstairs so that he might have a few more moments with the girl he was leaving behind him. From back of the curtain, shortly, she saw him swinging off down the hilly street in his erect way. Then, because no one came near the room, she stayed there at the window until she heard the long hoarse whistling of the down-river boat.

Chapter III

I T was summer now, and Omaha was a whirlpool
of movement with its influx of emigrants.

More skeletons of new homes and stores (for
saddlers, gunsmiths, whipmakers) were scattered up
and down the hill streets. Acres of sunflowers. yel-
lower than newly discovered Montana gold, surrounded the town and wandered through its vacant
blocks.

Hammering, sawing, the cracking of blacksnake
whips, creaking of covered wagons, steamboat whistling, bawling of cattle—these were the town's
sounds. Freshly cut cottonwood, belching coal smoke,
animal offal, fish, green-scummed mud-swamps—
these were the smells.

There were days when the sun shone burningly on
the hot blistered hills, cracks formed in the parched
earth, and a gray velvety dust lay thick on the town.
There were days when boiling black clouds swept
up the river valley, cracking thunder reverberated
through the Missouri hills, and the rain came, so
that carriage and Conestoga wagon alike wallowed
to the hubs in the black mud.

Far to the west new steel rails glistened in the
prairie sun. Forts were planned to go up through the

Powder River Country, the Sioux's best hunting ground, and Red Cloud and his warriors were waiting their day of retaliation.

To the north the Arikara were on the warpath for the Sioux. In the south the Comanches never ceased their raiding. All tribes everywhere milled about that summer, angered at the white man's encroachment, at the slaughter of the buffalo, at the steel rails pointing west.

But tales of this undercurrent of restlessness, filtering into the river town and hence to the Colsworth household via Uncle Henry and his meal-time monologues, affected the two girls very little. Nor did it worry Uncle Henry himself to any extent.

"Washington and the army will take care of the vermin," was his decision.

It was as though the order had been given by him personally and with finality, for he had great local events on his mind.

Was the territory of Nebraska to become a state or not? The Union-Republicans had worked for it, the Democrats against it. Uncle Henry had put in long hours behind closed doors with a few choice friends. The pro-state people had won, but with a list of election irregularities to be flung in their faces for decades to come. One precinct's votes had been thrown out entirely because the judges carted the locked ballotbox off with them to dinner for an hour.

But that was in the past, all smoothed over with subtle explanation by Uncle Henry. The territory of

Nebraska had voted to become a state. Now was coming the fight to try and retain the capital at Omaha. All those who had opposed statehood were spitefully throwing their energies toward its removal to the south side of the Platte River, which was more free from Indians and so less exposed to their depredations.

Uncle Henry's big two-part beard fairly pumped up and down as he related all the ins and outs of the fight to his three womenfolks. But they let it go in one ear and out the other, being far more interested in Cynthia's letters from Fort Leavenworth and the fact that a new manteau-maker had arrived in town than in the retention of the old white building up on the hill.

For that was the first year in which the young Omaha gave evidence of becoming social-minded. Now it was beginning to do something besides supply the emigrants' needs and quarrel over local issues.

The wives and daughters of the men who were making money began to give little parties in their homes. The Bachelors' Mess, where George Hemming and several other eligibles lived, gave a dance at the Hernden House. A group of the business and professional men and their families started holding a monthly dinner with dancing at the near-by towns of Florence and Bellevue. Cynthia and Linnie, with their contrasting coloring and their pretty mushroom dresses, were quite the belles at these functions.

So on this summer afternoon all were making

preparations for one of these affairs. Even Aunt Louise, with a new black silk and a gold chain long enough to stake out a horse to grass, thought she was feeling fit to go and look on. Uncle Henry, away with the bays on a short prairie trip, was to meet them in Bellevue, having delegated George Hemming to stop for the three women and deliver them safely to the hotel.

And then it was none other than Polly who had to throw the monkey-wrench into the well-oiled wheels of the plan. As though temperamental over such social goings-on, she drooped, hung her head, and finally flopped down to the cage floor in a spell which would have been called a faint in a human female.

Cynthia picked up her long skirts, tiptoed through the horse-barn and across the alley to get Olga but returned without her, angered that Olga had taken it upon herself to go somewhere. Although Polly got all right shortly, the excitement was too much for Aunt Louise.

"It's come," she said resignedly. "Get the hot packs."

So when George Hemming drove up with his matching roan team and shining harness, Linnie volunteered to be the one to stay.

Aunt Louise made weak little arguments against Linnie's staying behind when she was company, with Linnie saying bosh, she wasn't company if she was going to stay all winter. Then she put forth a slightly stronger argument against Cynthia's going alone with George, betrothed as she was to Lieutenant Stafford, with Cynthia saying she just couldn't sit around and twiddle her thumbs, and anyway Father would be there at the hotel, for there was no way to get word to him now to stop him.

So, knowing full well that her steadier services would be more effective than the flighty Cynthia's, and especially since Cynthia was entirely agreeable to the decision, Linnie remained behind. And Cynthia, betrothed or not, went off with George Hemming behind the prancing roans.

Linnie took hot packs back and forth for an hour or more to Aunt Louise in her bedroom with its walnut furniture, wash-bowl and pitcher, and fringed antimacassars. Then she heard the door-bell ring. Some one was turning the bell's knob frequently and impatiently, so that she hurried down to answer its irritable summons.

The man in uniform standing there on the stoop was breathing hard as though he had been walking up the long hill street at top speed.

"Why . . . Lieutenant Stafford!"

"Cynthia . . . is she . . . ?" Then, as though suddenly remembering the presence of this other young lady, he broke off and shook hands: "How do you do, Miss Linnie? Cynthia . . . is she here?"

"No, she isn't . . . not just now."

"Where will I find her?"

"She started for Bellevue an hour ago," adding with needless explanation, "Her father is with her."

"Bellevue!" he snapped his fingers in exasperation. "Why, we stopped there!"

"I'm so sorry. But won't you come in?" She was thankful that he could not know how his presence affected her.

He followed her into the front parlor, glanced about the room with hungry eyes as though to call back the sight of Cynthia in its gracious setting, looked searchingly at Linnie as though by some magic means she could produce her.

"Won't you be seated?"

"No, I'll have to get back to the boat. I'm sent up the river to keep navigation open. Indians are troublesome again farther up. I tried to get leave to stay over for the next boat, but I must accompany my men. I ran up while it's being refueled."

"I'm so sorry," was all Linnie could repeat, which was no better than Polly could have done.

"I guess I can't conceal my disappointment. I pictured her here all the way . . . in this very room. Someway it never occurred to me she might be gone."

"I'm so . . ." No, she wouldn't mouth that parrot phrase again. "She'll be so disappointed."

"I shouldn't say all this to you . . . things that I had intended for her alone. But I must. It might be weeks before she could hear from me." He was speaking earnestly, looking down at her in that direct way she remembered so well. "Tell her I'll write her from the first place I can do so, probably Sioux City; later Fort Randall. And tell her this: if we are to winter at Fort Randall—or near enough for her to join me while the boats are still running—I want her to come to me. I have my superior officer's good wishes. There will be some officers' wives there wherever we are. We can be married by a Protestant missionary who winters at the fort ... or the commissioner may come up ... or Father De Smet on his way down the river ... or the commanding officer."

It went through her mind that Priest or Protestant, military or civil servant, apparently it made no difference. It was Cynthia who counted.

"Make her see all this. I know you can. There's something about you—substantial, I guess it is. I would know to look in your face that you are a true friend to both of us."

He was fumbling somewhere under his military coat. "Give her this." It was a little black case, the two sides joined with a hook and catch. His picture, she thought. "And give her this." He was bringing forth a small white box. A ring, she could tell.

Linnie stood with the two objects, one in each hand, her fingers closed over them. And then, as though to convey more, much more, through the medium of this substantial person—this girl whose face told him she was a true friend to them both— he put his own hands over Linnie's tight little fists.

"Tell her I love her ... more than anything in this world. Tell her that. And give her this." He drew

Linnie up to him as though she were Cynthia, kissed her lips warmly, and was gone.

And Linnie stood there in the middle of the parlor, both hands at her throat, still holding the ring and the picture in them so tightly that the skin on their knuckles was white in the dusk.

Fully dressed, she waited up for Cynthia in their room, met her at the head of the stairway to forestall unimportant chatter.

"News, Cynthia." She was very proud of the casual tone. Well, she had practised it enough. "Your big lieutenant was here."

"Norman! Not Norman!" Cynthia squealed, partly in genuine surprise, partly that she had been caught in the mischievous act of being away.

"Sh!" Linnie pulled her into the bedroom and shut the door. "Your mother's probably asleep."

"Where is he now?"

"Gone."

"Gone? Well, I *must say* ..."

"He was only here a few minutes, while the steamboat was refueling. He's on his way up the river."

"Up the river? Where?"

"Sioux City and then Fort Randall."

"How did he look?"

"He looked ... very well."

"Begin at the beginning. Tell me everything."

"Well ... he rang the bell and I opened the door like this." She made foolish motions. "No, I turned the knob the other way ..."

"Oh, you silly! Go on faster."

"He told me several things to tell you. I'll deliver them just as exact as I can. He is ordered up the Missouri to keep navigation open. The Indians are troublesome. He doesn't know just where he is to stay for the winter. But if it turns out to be Fort Randall, as he thinks, he wants you to come." She was painstaking in picking out the items, telling them off on her fingers. "He said there will be some officers' wives there. He said there would be a Protestant missionary to marry you or Father De Smet or the commissioner or the commanding officer. He said he had his superior officer's good wishes. He was very anxious that you should be with him when he is settled for the winter. And he left three things for you."

She felt in the pocket of her flaring skirt with its galloon braid trimming. "He said to give you this." She brought out the picture case.

Cynthia opened it and squealed excitedly: "Oh, he is . . . yes, he *is* better looking than George Hemming, isn't he?"

"And this!" Linnie took from that same pocket the little white ring box.

Cynthia did not squeal this time. "Oh, Linnie, I don't like it so very well," she wailed. "I'd rather have one of those with a blue stone . . . and wider. What else?" She held out her hand. And when Linnie made no further move she said impatiently: "Go on. I want the other. You told me three things."

"Did I say three? That was stupid." She turned the big pocket of her skirt inside out. "See . . . that's all."

For the third thing was not in her pocket.

Chapter IV

IT was only a week later that a letter came down the river from Sioux City. Cynthia was in her usual excitement over its arrival and read it aloud glibly to Linnie. " 'I love you more than tongue can tell.' " Oh, how could she bear to let any one else know what was in it? " 'You are in my thoughts day and night and I live for the time we can be together.' "

It threw her into a feverish mood of preparation. What if Norman would send for her before all her new things were finished? Right in the heat of the summer she went down to the dry-goods stores nearly every day, coming back in a convulsed state to tell Linnie how George Hemming fell over himself to wait on her, joking her about the muslin and rickrack braid she was buying but acting sad about it, too.

Linnie and Aunt Louise were both helping with the sewing, and sometimes, when there was an end to her almost endless tasks, Olga helped, too.

Although a great cable joining two continents had just been laid and shining steel rails had crept slowly and painfully a few miles farther to the west, neither event was as significant to Cynthia as the awaited arrival of her next letter.

Two weeks went by and there was no word yet, with Cynthia more provoked than worried at the long delay.

It was hard for the girls to sew in the stifling heat which lay over the hilly town like a huge, smothering buffalo-hide.

Over at the Hernden House the guests sat out on the long porches in rockers, whacking at flies with their palm-leaf fans. Scarcely a day went by without its runaway, some fly-bitten horse plunging wildly down a hill street with careening buggy. Spring chickens, having escaped both the ax and their picketed yard, cuddled into the thick gray dust of residential streets. Cockle-burrs, sunflowers, and burdock wilted languidly in vacant lots. Some days Indian squaws begged at the Colsworth back door. Olga gave them cold pancakes with an uncharitable look thrown in for good measure.

On one of these hot afternoons, with the girls sewing on the side porch, Uncle Henry came driving home coatless, his collar wilted, and even his bristly whiskers drooping.

He had a piece of news. Word had come in that a band of Indians had swept down on a freight crew out at Plum Creek and captured the train. General Dodge had been out at the end of the line but had hooked on his private car to an engine and raced back to the scene with armed men. They had found the freight train burning, had fired on the Indians, and there had been quite a skirmish.

"Cynthia, if I thought there'd be any more trouble up around Fort Randall, I'd never let you set foot up there."

At his own words he jumped up and went into the house to come back with a letter for Cynthia. The letter which would tell about her coming!

"Why, Father... how *could* you forget it just for that old Indian uprising?"

Norman was up at Fort Randall, and, as he had said, several of the officers' wives were there. But now he was bitterly disappointed over what he had to tell her. If he had been going to stay she could have come before winter closed in, but they had just been ordered on up the river to Fort Berthold in the Dakota Territory. It was a long journey, and there would be no possibility of her coming that fall. In the spring, though, at the breaking of the ice when navigation would start again, she must come on one of the very first boats. Father De Smet was at Fort Berthold working among the tribes there, or the commanding officer could marry them. It would be a long time before they could see each other, but she must remember his deep love and how they would both be waiting for the ice to go out in the spring.

Cynthia was disappointed but not fatally, as her next words proved.

"Listen to this, Linnie," she squealed at the paragraph. " 'Though the ice will separate us, the river always runs below. That is like my love for you.' Do you know, Linnie, I actually don't believe George Hemming could write anything like that. Why, it sounds poetical, like Mr. Alfred Tennyson." She read it again in rhythmic fashion. " 'Though the ice will separate us . . . the river always runs below . . . the lady of Shalott.' See what I mean?"

The letter closed with all the love in his heart for her and his courteous regards to her parents and Linnie.

He had enclosed a hand-drawn map of the Missouri River and the forts which dotted it. Cynthia pinned it on the gilt wall-paper by the highboy so that the way of her potential journey would be there before her.

Sometimes, when she found herself alone in the bedroom, Linnie would stand for a few moments and look at the crude facsimile. It fired her imagination, that long line running its twisting northwest course with penciled spots for Fort Randall—Fort Pierre—Fort Rice—Fort Berthold. She pictured herself as Cynthia on one of those spring boats, uniformed soldiers all about her, passing Fort Randall, Fort Pierre, Fort Rice, then arriving at Fort Berthold and Norman Stafford meeting her. And after that to be with him always, to go wherever he was sent.

There was something peculiarly fascinating about the army life of which he had told her. She knew it must be hard and dangerous, but still it held an allure, at least it would if she could be with Norman Stafford. The very adventurousness of it appealed to her, the changes, the following the flag wherever it led. Deep in her heart she would wonder what quirk of fate had made Cynthia the one he loved while she had only his courteous regards. Then she would realize suddenly the audacity of her thinking and come back to the world of Uncle Henry and his household.

For Uncle Henry was in a constant foment over various events these days: the mismanagement of the Union-Republican convention (in which the party dropped its first name), President Johnson's blunders, the skulduggery of the territorial Democrats. He loudly read lengthy vindictive articles from the local papers in which leading citizens were frankly called names of barnyard origin.

The womenfolks, with true femininity, shuddered at the epithets, but also with true femininity of the times failed to understand (or care) from the stormy monologues just what he was for and against. All they knew was that, with a few choice cronies, he constantly held long secret sessions from which he emerged with plans to manipulate affairs in the coming legislature.

Then—and this affected Cynthia much more than the complicated politics for which she had no liking —her father began turning against Norman for his stubborn clinging to the army when he had been offered a good chance here in the coming city of the west.

"It's a wild goose chase . . . tagging an army man around. I supposed of course he'd jump at the chance to get into something here. There's money here. Figure it out for yourself. People have to eat. Put up a grocery store. They have to have buggies and harness. Buy into those businesses. They have to keep warm. Get into the wood and coal business. They need transportation. Get hold of railroad and steamboat stock. Town's full of young fellows who'll do all that and be worth a good deal some day."

In September black clouds rolled down the river valley, the rains came, and the hilly streets were morasses. No self-respecting team made any attempt to run away, their horse sense telling them they would not get far. The cottonwoods and the willows dripped clammily, and all the white sweet-williams and the blue sage and the wild phlox at the edge of town were gone. The two seminaries opened. Steamers hurriedly disgorged late supplies at the dock for the Union Pacific. There was a traveling show in the Academy of Music, the town's second story "opera house."

October came on, bringing a few days of squaw winter, that first cold spell which would not stay. Then followed days which the Indians called second summer, with a haze hanging about the Missouri valleys like smoke from the lodges of Chief Fontenelle's people, with great flocks of blackbirds flying across the sun and the sumac along the river-banks as red as any signal fires on the hillsides. A crowd of one hundred and fifty easterners arrived to hunt and to see the progress made by the shining new rails to the west. They came in sumptuous fashion, with a band, a photographer, cooks and caterers, provisions and rare wines. And Uncle Henry fairly blew up to the bursting point when he and the girls met and talked with some of the prominent ones during their brief stay.

Then the household moved again on its regular routine: Uncle Henry noisily arriving for his three big meals, leaving immediately afterward for the law office where almost everything was done except law. Aunt Louise planning to get out now, to make more friends and enter into the town's activities, only to fall back to the comfort of the horsehair sofa. Olga and Magnus coming across the alley from their small home early in the morning, performing their tasks with all the thoroughness of their Swedish training. Linnie and Cynthia doing the lighter work about the house in their wide-skirted morning prints with jet breastpins at their neat collars, dressing up in the afternoon and changing to gold breastpins, even though they only sat and sewed on Cynthia's quilts.

There was diversion from the monotony of all this in the occasional affairs which dotted the calendars of the town's socially inclined. The twins, Victoria and Virgilla, gave a little party in their home. There was a dance on one of the steamboats tied at the dock and a dinner at the hotel, with Cynthia and Linnie quite frankly the acknowledged belles.

Sometimes Cynthia confided to Linnie the daring things George Hemming said to her at the parties: that he would wager she was in love with a uniform instead of a man and that he didn't believe she would make a good army wife anyway; how he made her so angry she wouldn't speak to him all evening, just turned her head when they met in the dance, until he said something so funny she had to burst right out laughing.

November came in, bleak and gray. The last of the wild geese flew honking down the valley, and the last steamboat, like a lone goose paddling after them, left for St. Louis. The river froze and the snows came. Magnus butchered one of the two hogs and Olga rendered lard, made sausage and headcheese, and pickled the feet, using everything but the "ears, tail and sqveal," she said.

In the middle of the month came the first letters from Norman. Three of them at one time arrived by stage, as the mail was sent now from Fort Berthold by Indian runner to Virginia City or Helena in the Montana territory, thence to Omaha by overland stage. They had been over a month on the way. Cynthia said it just terrified her to read how much he thought of her.

Then there was no more word until a few days before Christmas. This time there was only one letter, but Cynthia was all excitement to read in it that, if all went well with the mails, a gift he had arranged for would be delivered to her door on the day before Christmas, and when she saw it she would know how much he loved her and wanted her.

When that day came, she could scarcely take her eyes from the street, so that when a boy arrived in the late afternoon she was ready to meet him at the door.

To her surprise it was only an envelop which he handed her, and the gift turned out to be a paid passage to Fort Berthold, good on any of the boats owned by the steamboat company in question: the *Waverly*, the *River Rose*, the *Deer Lodge*, and others. A note from the company asked Miss Colsworth to get in touch with the steamboat depot in the early spring and they could give her more information about the first running of the boats.

"What a queer present!" She was quite frank in her appraisal. "When you stop to think about it, it's really just a piece of paper. You can't wear it or get one bit of good from it for such a long time from now."

Then she drew Linnie into their bedroom with secretive gestures and opened the bottom drawer of the highboy. "Look, Linnie! George Hemming gave me this." A wide black-and-gold bracelet with gold padlocked clasp lay in its purple velvet box. "But I'm not going to tell the folks."

"Oh, Cynthia, you're not?"

"They're so old-fashioned, they would have a fit

and fall in it . . . presents from two young men at one time."

"I'll wager they wouldn't like you to take jewelry from a man not your betrothed."

"Pooh! These are the late eighteen-sixties, not those old early forties when they were young. As good luck would have it, Mother was in bed and Olga not here, so no one knows about the steamboat papers but you. I'm not going to mention them, and they'll just take it for granted the bracelet is a betrothal present from Norman. If they say anything to you about it, promise me you'll pretend you got it from the post-office when you went downtown yesterday."

"Oh, Cynthia, I couldn't. . . ."

"Oh, you prissy!" Cynthia's amiability had fallen from her like a shawl. "You say one word to the folks about this bracelet coming from George and I'll tell a few things about you. Don't think I haven't seen you stand and moon over Norman's picture and . . ."

"Cynthia!"

"See . . . you're blushing."

"Who wouldn't blush at such a bold-faced . . ."

But Cynthia had picked up the fallen shawl of her amiability and was laughing a little self-consciously. "Anyway," she wheedled, "promise you'll try and help your cousin out of a hole."

"At least I'll not deliberately push you in," Linnie said dryly and walked out of the room, deeply perturbed. Oh, what had Cynthia said!

January arrived and the Missouri River was frozen solid. Great snows were banked high with winds coming down from the north like so many Sioux warriors. The female population of the community was shut in, more or less, so that all three women in the Colsworth home spent much of their time with Cynthia's sewing. Chemises. Petticoats with rickrack edging on countless tucked ruffles. Quilts— plain squares and the "orange peel" and Olga's "floo-de-liss"—with Uncle Henry saying dryly the government would probably order that kind now for the whole army, and as far as he was concerned, unless Norman Stafford stopped his foolishness and resigned, he didn't deserve them.

Olga fought her way through the deep snow every day, and Magnus curried the rough winter coats of the bays until they were reddish-brown silk. The girls cleaned Polly's cage, dusted Mozart in the parlor and sad Lincoln in the back parlor, and did all the bedroom work. On those days when Olga was washing in the steamy kitchen, or ironing multitudinous flounces and table-cloths into glazed perfection, they brought the potatoes and the squash from the dirt cellar and prepared them, strained the sour milk through a clean cloth for Dutch cheese, polished and trimmed the coal-oil lamps and washed the chimney of the new hanging one over the dining-room table.

By two o'clock they were always ready for the sewing. Unless she was enjoying one of her bad spells, Aunt Louise, with her little bloodless feet on a warm soapstone, made all the buttonholes in her precise way.

Uncle Henry was wrapped in the doings of the last territorial legislature, which was convening in Omaha. It was asking for a new military post in the southwestern part as protection against the Indians, and, what was more important locally, authorizing the construction of a railway bridge across the river. It ended in a fine display of emotion when a legislator drew his pistol and another his sword at the end of a strongly worded argument. But as there was no massacre, the last territorial session finished with a semblance of peace.

Only a few times did the girls get out-of-doors that month. But when the wild winds abated after blowing the snow off the river in irregular paths, Uncle Henry took them and their friends, Victoria and Virgilla, in the double-seated cutter, across to the Iowa side where others of the citizenry were driving, too, like so many Israelites crossing a frozen Red Sea.

The tracks of the Chicago and Northwestern Railroad had been finished from Denison, Iowa, and the first train puffed into Council Bluffs. No longer would one need to take the creaking old stage as the girls had done on their return from the east. All Council Bluffs was celebrating with music, parades, and a speech by General Dodge.

They had dinner at the hotel, with Uncle Henry calling for the most expensive of everything for his guests. Uncle Henry was at his noisiest best when bestowing largess upon those around him. When he gave, he gave not only freely but loudly, with much attention to the giver.

The bitterly cold month was passing, and no letter had come from Norman, that mid-December letter remaining the last Cynthia had received. She chafed under the silence, cried a little at the neglect, with Linnie assuring her she would soon hear. But many times when Cynthia was unaware of it, Linnie looked to the north as though the ice-bound distance could tell the mystery of what lay beyond, even while she censured herself for the interest which was deeper than sympathy for Cynthia.

Then the stage got through from Montana territory to North Platte, where already the Union Pacific was running trains, and three letters came in over those shining new rails which had been laid for so dear a price. And the central theme of all three letters was Cynthia's coming to Fort Berthold by the first boat in the spring.

February! And winter, the pugilist, lessened its stranglehold on the Nebraska Territory. Water started to run in little yellow streams down the hilly streets over old layers of ice. Uncle Henry refused to ride on the softening river. The girls received any number of valentines in the way of sentimental poetry from the town's young blades.

A seamstress came to the house every day, sewing like mad. She had a mannish-looking hard face, but the things she turned out were marvels of intricate feminine furbelows. A room upstairs had been set aside for her, but scraps of cloth, thread and yarn, braid, buttons, paper patterns, pins, and whalebones oozed out and down the stairway into every room.

Several times now the girls went downtown together shopping, stepping over the miniature creeks. They held their dresses discreetly at the ankle's lowest boundary line, never glancing toward a barbershop, turning their heads quickly if any of those orange-haired women passed by, although they confided to each other they would just admire to do the opposite of every one of those things sometime and see what would happen.

When they went into the dry-goods store, George Hemming always managed to shunt his current customer to another clerk and take charge, keeping Cynthia in such a state of convulsion that she could scarcely tell galloon braid from soutache.

On one of these mild days Linnie began to talk at the dinner-table about her year being over, that soon now she would go to Sioux City to visit the girlhood friend who lived there, saying before them all that she and Cynthia could travel together on the same boat as far as Sioux City. Uncle Henry said he wasn't sure Cynthia was going to go on that wild-goose journey at all.

Cynthia flared up: "*That's* a pretty thing to say when I've got my sewing all done and Norman sent..." She broke off and turned red, looking guiltily at Linnie over the secret of the paid passage.

"Sewing or no sewing," Uncle Henry said loudly, "we're going to wait and see what the damn Indians are up to."

Polly called out raucously, "Fit to kill." Olga scuttled out to the kitchen to Magnus. And Aunt Louise put her hand to her head and told the girls to get the hot packs ready.

Chapter V

THE first of March came in, and now after years of agitation and heated quarreling the old Nebraska territory was a state, for President Johnson, with some delay over civil rights wording, had signed the decree.

Although there was no official celebration, Uncle Henry and a few choice souls solemnized the date later in his back office, the joy of their convivial rites tempered by the knowledge that the capital itself was to be moved from Omaha, the majority of the legislators having so decreed. Uncle Henry told the womenfolks frankly there were times when the majority acted like jackasses, so that they all jumped at the strong language.

The new capital was to be named Lincoln. The irony of the whole thing was that, because the legislators who had led the fight for the removal had been opposed to President Lincoln, those members who wished to keep the capital at Omaha had moved to name the new and as yet unfounded town Lincoln, with the bright thought that the others would oppose a place so named. But the bright idea had backfired, and now this coming summer the committee was to choose the site of Lincoln, the new capital city (according to Uncle Henry's terse phrase), "in some God-forsaken spot out on the prairie."

All this bored Cynthia to distraction. "Who cares about the old white capitol on the hill?" she asked irritably. "And state or territory . . . I don't feel one bit different."

It had been weeks since she had heard from Norman, and she was less worried now than angry.

Linnie spoke her own fears: "Did you ever think that something could have happened?"

"Oh, pooh! Nothing has happened. He just isn't being nice to me. *I'm* the one who is doing everything to get ready . . . seeing to all my clothes. Or do you think something has happened?" She burst into tears. "Oh, Linnie, I'm so miserable."

Love was not like that. Love was loyalty. It was deep and abiding. It was like the river under its icebound surface, running below. Army wives had to have faith in their men. Army wives had to wait—and watch—and wait some more, without question. Some way she knew intuitively how an army wife would have to be different from other wives.

Suddenly winter returned. All the little streams congealed again as though a giant hand, held up before them, had bade them cease their flowing. The snows came, thick and blinding, and of all the women only strong Swedish Olga and the hard old dressmaker bucked the blizzards.

On an early afternoon with the sun out again from behind deflated clouds, sidewalks cleared and paths partly shoveled, Cynthia went downtown to get more thread and rickrack braid for the sewing. She looked very pretty in her dark mantle, fur-trimmed muff, and winter bonnet with red ribbon against her light hair.

All afternoon Linnie and Aunt Louise basted multitudinous yards of ruffling by hand, and the dressmaker pedaled the new Singer machine. The pale sunshine flickered out, the dressmaker went home, and Cynthia had not come.

Uncle Henry jinglingly arrived in the cutter, coming in the back way, stomping snow. Only a few moments later there was more sleighbell-jingling at the front of the house. Then the big door opened and Cynthia, too, was stomping snow on the threshold of the hall. And George Hemming was with her.

They came on through to the back parlor where George, with no preliminary training in a tactful approach to Aunt Louise, blurted it out: "Get ready for the surprise. We're married. Meet Mr. and Mrs. George Hemming." This was the joke supreme.

Cynthia's voice was a mixture of gaiety and fear. "Yes, it's true." She giggled nervously.

The bridegroom laughed, too, but, in the face of Aunt Louise's pallor, not spiritedly.

Before any one could come out of the awful silence into which the news had thrown them, Cynthia was explaining in a high tense voice: "George is going clear to Chicago to-morrow. The store's sending him and paying his way. They say no more depending on drummers for everything. He wanted me to marry him and go with him."

As long as she lived Linnie never would forget the confusion of the hour which followed. Aunt Louise, clutching her heart and taking to the sofa. Uncle Henry, striding about the room, scolding and blowing, apparently more provoked that it had been done in this way than that it had been done at all, reminding them that a lot of people knew about Cynthia's betrothal and that they could expect unfriendly gossip. George, trying to explain further how the great joke came about. Cynthia, breaking into nervous crying. Olga, coming to the dining-room to set the table and scuttling back to the kitchen and Magnus in excitement. Polly, moved to a frenzy by the commotion, jumping from the perch to the floor of her cage and back again, with her raucous "Ha! Ha! Fit to kill."

Linnie, standing back of the perturbed family circle, kept thinking of only one thing: what about Norman? While all the loud words surged around and about her like high spring waters, only one thought was uppermost: Norman. One feeling took precedence over all others: sympathy for Norman. Sympathy—and something else. Something new and strangely stirring. Something approaching an exciting light-heartedness.

For a time the storm raged, but gradually Uncle Henry calmed down. While the bride and Linnie were putting hot packs on Aunt Louise, and Olga was frantically trying to change a fried-potato supper into a wedding feast, Uncle Henry began to tell George the news which had just come in that afternoon, about the government buying that hunk of ice up in the corner of the world called Alaska, and saying that all the fools weren't dead yet.

George laughed so uproariously at Uncle Henry that Uncle Henry swelled visibly, and by the time Olga's very good meal was over and his new son-in-law had told some funny jokes, Uncle Henry seemed quite affable.

"Well, one thing, Mother." He settled back in portly comfort. "She won't be trying to follow the army all around Robin Hood's barn."

Aunt Louise, taking her cue from his changing attitude, echoed that she, too, was glad to think her girl wouldn't have to follow the army all around Robin Hood's barn. Cynthia flushed and began to talk about something else.

After supper the two girls came together in embarrassed silence in the upstairs hall.

It was Cynthia who broke the strained quiet. "Linnie, I know what you're thinking." She clutched at her sleeve. "I'm sorry for Norman. He'll take it hard, won't he? But I couldn't marry them both, could I? And if Norman wouldn't write to me . . . *I'm* the one that should be angry, shouldn't I? But I'm not. I still love him. I even think you can love two people, don't you? But you can't *marry* two people, can you? And what do you think George said?

'All's fair in love and war, but it's only the war that's over.' Wasn't that funny?"

Linnie said nothing, only stood looking at the girl who could chatter about a love that was not loyalty.

When she continued her silence, Cynthia went on: "Help me pack, will you? That's a dear! I'm lucky to have all my new things, but George says when I get to Chicago I can pick out goods for another dress. Linnie, I'd admire to have green this time ... a deep green silk with ..."

Linnie put her hands on the girl's shoulders and gave them a sudden shake. "Cynthia! You must write him at once ... to-night ... before you go. Spring is almost here. He'll be waiting for you."

That paradoxical feeling of sympathy and elation was flooding her. He will take it hard ... but he isn't Cynthia's any more. He will be terribly hurt ... but he is free.

Cynthia's lip quivered and there was a faint suggestion of tears. "Linnie, you write it to him."

"Oh, I *couldn't* do that."

"Yes, you could. I couldn't bear to hurt him. And tell him I forgive him for not writing. I just can't be angry at him now."

"Oh ... Cynthia ... how could you do it to him?"

"You tell him. Please! And send him back the things he gave me. But stand up for me, Linnie, so he'll see I couldn't help it. You'll do that, won't you?"

"Oh, Cynthia! Cynthia!"

"Promise me you'll tell him."

"I . . . promise."

There was scant time to dwell on the import of Cynthia's sudden marriage, with all the getting ready and packing for the journey which must follow.

It took many satchels and hatboxes to get Cynthia off, and what with her excitement over finding herself a bride, Aunt Louise's general bewilderment, and Olga waiting on every one with frantic haste, Linnie was manager of those hurried preparations.

Quite a large group went down to the stage depot to see the newly married couple off. But the stage trip now would be a mere crossing of the ice to the Iowa side and on to the new depot in Council Bluffs. No longer did one have to bounce around in the creaking vehicle all that long trip to Denison. Not a month but made Omaha more like an eastern city, Uncle Henry said.

Cynthia and George were very gay and highly pleased with their new status. Cynthia was all in maroon, with the new broadcloth manteau and matching hat, which ironically she had intended to wear up the river to Fort Berthold. George had a canceled railroad ticket with which he was anticipating fooling the conductor for a time.

Victoria and Virgilla were there and, like the villagers on the green, several of George's bachelor friends. These with Uncle Henry, Aunt Louise, and Linnie made a fair-sized crowd. It was an extravagant adventure for Aunt Louise, but she would go to bed as soon as she got home. In the midst of the healthy youth of the crowd and Uncle Henry's animal strength she looked as flat and delicate as one of the velvet pansies on the black bonnet whose ribbon strings, tied behind her ears, accentuated their size.

Uncle Henry was in fine fettle this morning, dominating the scene and carrying on much of the conversation. One might have picked him for the bridegroom.

Just before the stage was leaving, with the frosty air full of good-bys and Cynthia already going up the steps, a peculiar thing happened. Linnie, standing close to Uncle Henry, saw him shake hands with George in farewell, and then for the brief space of a moment sensed something passing between them and overheard a fragmentary conversation about the whole thing turning out well. In reality it was only a gesture and some mumbled words which she could not swear she had heard aright. But, surprisingly, it seemed in that brief second that Uncle Henry and George knew something which no other human being knew.

Over and over on the way home she pondered that flash of understanding she had witnessed, was to do so many times in her life, always wondering but never to know the answer. Did Uncle Henry have knowledge of that sudden marriage before it occurred? So many of the little pieces fitted together. The things he had said about the army. Norman's refusal to give it up and settle down in Omaha. The time getting close for Cynthia to go. The combination of her stubbornness and indecision. George's eligibility and his promise of being a money-maker. Uncle Henry's ability to do things behind closed doors. His stormy attitude when the elopers came home but his almost miraculous change. Not knowing for sure, still the impression was so strong and startling that it gave her a queer feeling of distress and distrust.

The house was very quiet now after Uncle Henry's and George's noisiness, with Olga slipping about quietly at her work and Polly sulking on the floor of her cage.

Linnie helped Aunt Louise to bed, picked up debris after the domestic hurricane, and then went to the room she had shared so long with Cynthia and would share no more. Seating herself at the little writing desk, she sat idly looking out toward the river. Poor Norman! What would he think and do? How could he comprehend such disloyalty? She must write the letter at once as she had promised. She could even carry it with her by boat up to Sioux City and send it on to him from there. It would be as though, out of her sympathy and loyalty, she were carrying it personally part-way to him.

As soon as the ice went out she would leave, visit Jessie (the seminary friend), and then go back east. It was really home back there, she told herself, but there was something out here in the new west which held her fancy. She tried to decide just what it was:

wide horizons, a sense of lusty growth all about her, the feeling that adventure might be just around the corner. Involuntarily her eyes sought the map on the wall, remembering again a man's disappointment and bitterness.

She picked up her slim gold pen. *To Lieutenant Stafford. Honored Friend. Friend Norman.* She tried different openings, could not get started. This message to arrive instead of Cynthia herself! How could one tell him so cruel a thing? Last night she had even thought there might be some pleasure and satisfaction in writing it, but there was neither. And perhaps there was no need for a letter at all. Those many weeks of silence! Perhaps something *had* happened.

She got up and walked over to the high-boy, standing before the map he had sketched. The long penciled line twisted and turned like the various emotions in a person's life. Omaha—Sioux City—Fort Randall—Fort Pierre—Fort Rice—Fort Berthold. She read them over so many times that the names became rhythmical like the words of a song.

Chapter VI

WILD geese flew honking up the valley, high over
the rolling hills. The streets ran yellow
water. Willows in the swamps swelled under the
prairie sun. The cottonwoods' tightly rolled buds re-
laxed. A million sunflower seeds stirred in their
black beds. Uncle Henry said Magnus could start
wheeling away the stable-straw packing around the
foundation of the house.

In the middle of a night Linnie sat up, startled
awake by the far-off sound of artillery. But it was not
guns. It was the ice, cracking and breaking with a
great hollow booming which reverberated among the
low-lying hills. *The ice is going out and the river
runs below,* she thought. And no letter had been
written to tell Norman Stafford that love was not
like the river underneath the ice—love was not
loyalty.

All night the ice groaned and snapped and piled
up during the travail of the river.

At breakfast Linnie told the folks it would soon
be time now for the boats to start, and she would be
leaving. Uncle Henry said a great deal very em-
phatically about her staying and being a second

daughter. Aunt Louise, like a languid echo, said, "Yes . . . stay and be a second daughter."

But Linnie told them that was not necessary when their own girl would be back so very soon and was going to live right here with them—for this the newly weds were planning to do.

I just couldn't stand it to have to laugh at George every day was what she was thinking but did not dare say. Norman Stafford was the only one she knew who would have grinned with her about that.

After breakfast she looked in the St. Louis paper to see if she could get any information about the boats. Mail from down the river still came from St. Joseph by stage. The boats were evidently starting. There were advertisements of the fine qualities of the *Deer Lodge*, the *River Rose*, the *Waverly*, a dozen more, and recommendations by former satisfied passengers.

It was queer to go downtown without Cynthia, for they had always been together. She hurried along almost in embarrassment to be unaccompanied, looking to neither right nor left, picking her way down through the deep slush to the steamboat depot.

It was early for the boats, they told her, but she could look for one within the week, they were sure.

At home again she packed her trunk and part of the two satchels and the three big hatboxes with the flowered wall-paper coverings, so that everything would be ready when a boat came.

It was the afternoon of the twenty-fifth of the

month, when she heard the long-drawn-out whistling and from her bedroom window could see people hurrying toward the dock. But for knowing the reason she would have thought the crowds were going to a fire. A late snow was falling but appeared to be melting as it came.

There was a great deal of importance and hoarse commotion about the boat's docking. Only a few minutes later the door-bell rang and a breathless young man was asking Linnie's company for the evening at a dance on the *Waverly*. Scarcely had he made his speech before another gallant arrived for the same purpose.

She was trying to handle the scene with diplomacy when Uncle Henry himself arrived to tell her the boat was in.

But there was no dance on the *Waverly*. And Linnie did not go to Sioux City on it. It was loaded to the guards with a detachment of Regular Army officers and soldiers. Business came before pleasure, and the business was the so-and-so Indians in the Sioux country. After refueling, the boat went on that very evening, for the new moon was up and the river high.

It was only two days later that the *River Rose* came. There was to be no dance this time either, the captain wanting to take advantage of the moon and the high water. So Uncle Henry came driving hurriedly in his cutter through the dirty snow to tell her they were going right on that same afternoon, but the captain had said he would wait for her. A high-boxed dray with shaggy-footed horses followed later for all the baggage.

Linnie dressed for the trip as fast as she could, her fingers all thumbs, lacing her high shoes and combing her long hair. She wore her green plaid wool, her new silk manteau, and her butter-bowl hat with its flat velvet bows. Hanging from her wrist with heavy black cord was a bag made from the same goods as her dress. She looked stylish and pretty and vibrant with youthful excitement over the coming journey.

Now that the time had come, she felt saddened to leave. Omaha, as new and uncouth as the young city was, had a lusty charm all its own. And so many things had happened here, among them several proposals of marriage which she had refused so graciously that two of the young men, thinking she only half meant it, had come back for more dismissals.

Suddenly she felt a warmness of heart for Uncle Henry and his loud high-handed ways, for Aunt Louise and her timorous little echoes, and for Cynthia fluttering around the tips of the blossoms of her childish pleasures. She felt a renewed kindliness for Olga and Magnus, so substantial and comfortable at their homely tasks, even for George who would number new birthdays with the passing years but would never grow up. At this moment of leaving she felt maternal, older than all of them, as old as humanity.

Her last act was to go back upstairs to say a hasty

good-by to the bedroom with its two wide windows looking toward the river. So much had happened here. Or had it? After all, thoughts were not happenings.

For only a moment she hesitated, then she crossed over to the high-boy and unpinned the river map. From the second drawer she took an inlaid handkerchief-box with a mirror in its top, extracted the steamboat-passage papers, and put them in the bag that hung from her wrist.

She came downstairs then and kissed Aunt Louise, who went suddenly tearful, so that Olga said she would put her to bed as soon as Linnie had gone. Polly thumped her old claws up and down on the floor of her cage and croaked: "So sorry!"

In the cutter Uncle Henry took the lines. Magnus untied the bays from the hitching-post, and they sprang away in the mud and slush.

"One of those days you can't tell whether to use a buggy or a cutter," Uncle Henry grumbled.

She waved back at frail Aunt Louise and sturdy Olga standing together in the front doorway, not knowing how much was to happen before she would see them again.

On the way the subject Linnie most dreaded came up.

"I'll pay your passage to Sioux City," Uncle Henry said.

"I have my passage," she said quietly.

That was all right with Uncle Henry. He did not

even question it. Linnie had been down to the steamboat office, and she had money of her own.

The freshly painted *River Rose* towered above the dock like a white-frosted birthday cake with smoke-stacks for candles. Passengers swarmed on her decks or strolled up and down the levee.

They went on board at once and found the young woman with whom Linnie had to share a stateroom, a plump little person who was going on up to Fort Rice.

"Now don't worry about anything," Uncle Henry said cheerfully in farewell. "Not many steamboat accidents any more."

A tall gaunt woman with a weather-beaten face, standing just back of them, heard him. "The *Louisville's* layin' under water at Pratt's cut-off," she said dryly with the hard twang of a crow. "The *Mollie Dozier's* got her pretty hulk down in the snags below Council Bluffs. The *Kansas* is down by Linden Landing and the *Kate Sweeny's* by Vermilion River. The *Nugget* won't never come up again, ner the *Ontario* near Kansas Bend, ner the *Tempest*. No more will the *General Grant* three mile below Bellevue ner the old sidewheeler *Gus Linn*." They both stood staring at the woman, not wanting to listen but not able to do otherwise. "The river gets 'em all," she finished laconically and walked away.

Uncle Henry shrugged impatiently. "Old harpy! Don't have anything to do with her."

He gave Linnie a whiskery kiss and a copy of

Barnaby Rudge for diversion on the way and went down the gang-plank.

She waved discreetly to him while the boat backed away from the levee into midstream. The last thing she saw of him shocked her immeasurably. He was nodding quite amiably to one of those orange-haired women.

But now she was forgetting all that in the interest of settling in the stateroom she must share with the plump little woman for the two or more days it would take to get to Sioux City. One never knew how long it would take to get anywhere on a steamboat on the Missouri, the woman said. Sand-bars, snags, the changing channel, shifting sand, it was the most changeable river in the whole country.

" 'Just like a woman,' my husband says. But one thing, we've got a good pilot—none better. Did you see him up in his little house on the roof of the saloon between the two high funnels where he can look down? That was his wife, that tall thin woman who was telling you about the sunken steamers. She goes on every trip with him."

The room-mate's name was Mrs. Duncliff, and her husband was a lieutenant stationed at Fort Rice. During the short time in which Linnie was disposing of the belongings from her satchel she learned that Mrs. Duncliff liked to travel on a boat better than the steam cars, that blue was her favorite color and *Beautiful Dreamer* her favorite song, that her husband had commanded a regiment of volunteers in the war but was now with the Regulars even though he had to step back to being a second lieutenant.

"The army just gets in the blood, I guess." She laughed.

By the time this information had been given gratuitously, the little lady decided it was time to know more about Linnie.

"Are you visiting up the river?"

"Yes."

"A lieutenant's wife?"

"No."

"A captain's?"

"No." She smiled across at her questioner.

"A major's?"

"No."

"Don't tell me it's a *colonel's* wife?"

Linnie laughed outright at that, and the little lady laughed with her, so that in the friendly merriment it went unanswered.

Out on deck with Mrs. Duncliff, she found a heterogeneous lot of passengers, preponderantly masculine. Besides the two of them there were only five other women on board, Mrs. Duncliff told her: two miners' wives and a merchant's wife, who were going into the mountains to join their husbands, and that gaunt somber woman, the pilot's wife. She seemed to be everywhere on the boat, apparently having access to any part of it. The pilots were highly paid, Mrs. Duncliff said, and the wife no menial. But looking at the woman's red chapped face and rough hands and then glancing down at her own soft skin, Linnie wondered how any woman could allow herself to become so weather-beaten. And of course no real lady would.

The fifth woman Linnie did not see, for she was staying in her stateroom, ill since starting from St. Louis. She was a full-blooded Indian of the Blackfoot tribe, a chief's daughter, married to the white-whiskered elderly man who spent much of his time at the bar. He was a fur trader and very wealthy, so Mrs. Duncliff said. They had educated their children in the states and were now returning from a visit to them and a tour among the large cities of the country. The young boy who was here, there, and everywhere on the boat, teasing passengers and crew alike, was the couple's youngest, and a merchant from St. Louis going up to Montana Territory had dubbed him H. T., meaning Holy Terror.

Curiously, Linnie looked about the floating hotel which would be her temporary home.

The saloon was in the middle of the boat, and the cabins opened into it on both sides. A glass door opened from each cabin to a gallery, and there were two good-sized decks outside each end of the saloon.

A stairway led to the roof, and Linnie suggested going up there but changed her mind when Mrs. Duncliff showed her a hole in her dress, burned there by flaming cinders falling from the funnels.

To-day the old Missouri was very high and very muddy. It seethed and surged along its claylike banks and flowed darkly through adjoining timberland. There were places where it roared with a quickening of its waters, other places where it quieted down to a calmness, only to rush out again in a wild frenzy of cross-currents.

With a wool shawl under her more stylish manteau, Linnie sat on deck much of the time that afternoon watching the sunlight on the river, finding that even though it strove to do so, its beams could not penetrate below those tawny waters. She felt her face burning from the sharp spring breeze and grew fearful that by the time Sioux City came in sight she would have a memento of the trip—sunburn or freckles, both equally distasteful. She certainly didn't want to look like that pilot's weather-beaten wife and smiled a bit smugly at the comparison.

The elderly captain came and stopped in front of her deck-chair.

"Let's see, now." He had the self-assurance of a man of affairs and a paternal attitude toward this pretty passenger. "You're the young lady for Fort Berthold?"

Linnie raised wide brown eyes to his.

"My passage is paid for there . . . but"—it sounded as much like a question as a statement—"I'll probably get off at Sioux City."

"Well . . . well!" He puzzled a minute over that vague answer, touched his cap, and went away.

People usually knew their own business, his look implied, but this was something new. Maybe he'd better keep an eye on her. Decent young women didn't run around on Missouri River steamboats unsure of their destination.

The ladies had their supper at the captain's table with the officers of the boat. The waiters were all Negroes. Linnie was glad it was Mrs. Duncliff with whom she roomed. The others might have been good women, but they were uncouth and not quite tidy. They ate heartily like men, not in the dainty way she had been taught.

The old captain was a combination of dignity and loquaciousness, with an anecdote for every possible subject.

Some one spoke of the muddiness of the Missouri.

"That reminds me of what my old friend Thomas Hart Benton used to say, that the Missouri River water was a little too thick to swim in and not quite thick enough to walk on."

He knew the river and its tributaries like a book, the legends of the Indian tribes along its waters and the history of its villages. But strangely enough, he did not love it. It was an enemy to fight and conquer and to taunt when the journey was over.

Back on the deck next day, Linnie drew away by herself, shunning even the pleasant but talkative Mrs. Duncliff, so that she might think out this thing which had been haunting her for so long.

All day she tried to set her mind to the decision. There was no use evading it. She wanted to see Norman Stafford before she returned east.

She could not tell why it had been so persistent but there it was—a feeling that some momentous thing had been arranged for her. To have purchased her own passage for Fort Berthold was unthinkable. But to have the passage fall into her possession as it had seemed almost the answer to the wild thought which had been running through her mind ever since the day she could not bring herself to write the letter. To tell him about it herself. To go up the river where he was. To put her hand on his arm and say: "She's married. You mustn't feel too hurt. She's childish ... she doesn't know what loyalty is ... and if she doesn't know what loyalty is, why then she doesn't know what love is."

No, how silly! She couldn't say that. But she could tell him and then come back. She had gold-pieces in the little chamois bag under her stays. The passage up the river was paid. Her own money would pay her way back.

She took out the hand-drawn map again for the dozenth time. Sioux City. Then Fort Randall. That was up the river a few inches. Fort Pierre was about that much farther. She faltered a little over the longer distance from Fort Pierre to Fort Berthold. That really did look a long way up into the Dakota territory.

But she was quite free. Uncle Henry and Aunt Louise thought she was visiting in Sioux City several weeks and then going on east. Uncle David and Aunt Margaret didn't know she had started. There was

something both complicated and simple about it—
both irrational and reasonable—as though she were
suspended in between places and time and events. She
knew she should not do this wild thing—and yet she
might. She believed that when they sighted Sioux City
she would gather her things together and go down
the gang-plank—half-admitted that she was going
to stay on board.

She shook herself. Who ever heard of such a fantastic thing? Still, this was a modern age. The war
had made lots of changes in ladies. Nobody had
been able to stop Louisa Alcott and Clara Barton
and some of those modern women from doing what
they thought was right. And this was right. This was
so right that it was as though something beyond and
outside herself willed it. You didn't have to belong to
your relatives, body and soul. You could do things
with your own life if you had enough courage.

Promise me you'll be the one to tell him. I promise.

So back and forth went her argument and coun-
ter-argument, reasons offered but without decisions.

And there, on the morning of the third day just
as the captain had predicted, was the little town of
Sioux City. Because the spring water was not shallow
anywhere the usual delays with sand-bars and snags
had been at a minimum.

The captain came around to Linnie's deck-chair
now. Plainly this pretty young conundrum needed
looking after. When he saw that she had no appear-

ance of a passenger about to disembark, he questioned: "You're going upriver then?"

"Yes."

And now she was not doing things with her own life. Life was doing things to her.

Mrs. Duncliff wanted to go ashore to get material for a sunbonnet. Linnie had never possessed one, but she accompanied her roommate and returned to the boat with blue checked gingham for herself, so that soon she would have ample protection from the sun on the water.

Every one had been eager for news, from which they had been cut off for these three days. When the male passengers returned, much of their conversation was about President Johnson's having vetoed the civil rights bill. There were several hot arguments on deck. A southern song was started. A northern one outshouted it. A fight ensued until the captain came forward to put an end to the fracas. Apparently a captain was king on his own boat.

"I thought we were through with the fighting," Linnie said in exasperation.

"Oh, I guess men will always fight," her deckmate answered, "'til us women get a little say-so. Then there won't be any more fussing."

While the two women stood far back from the milling men, the pilot's wife came toward them, her green sunbonnet casting a peculiar hue across her thin dark face. Without preliminaries she said: "I go back and forth with my man. You never can tell.

Snags. Fire. Ice. Rocks. Injuns. Explosions. Sand-
bars."

They made polite, if brief, comments and went on
to the stateroom to cut out their own new sunbonnets.

The *River Rose* started upstream. There was no
turning back now. The die was cast.

That afternoon Linnie Colsworth wrote in her
diary—so yellowed now after three-quarters of a
century—*We have just passed Sioux City. I am on
my way to Fort Berthold.*

They traveled slowly all night, for the bright
moon was up and the river high.

Lying there in her bunk she slept fitfully. The en-
gines pounded out their steady rhythm, so that even
in her light sleeping she heard them.

All night they pounded it: *Chug chug…Fort
Randall…chug chug…Fort Pierre…chug chug
…Fort Rice…chug chug…Fort Berthold.*

Chapter VII

THERE was a great bend in the river now, and it was not so deep. It swept to the west as well as north, a vagrant gipsy of a river forever wandering where it willed, a river so wayward and perverse that it spent years building up its own banks only to tear them down again in a moment of wild frenzy.

Every night they tied up to the bank or to a protruding bar, for the moon had deserted them and the stars' pale light was not enough for travel. So young was the spring up here that patches of ice sometimes still lay in the shallow coves.

It took five more days to get to Fort Randall. They could see the buildings of the post through the timberland that bordered the river. Seemingly it was on the very edge of civilization. The captain said they would be here quite a while as he must dicker for wood. Later they saw him arguing with the woodchoppers at the side of the long corded piles on the bank.

The commanding officer of the fort came on board and asked the ladies if they would like to go on shore for the time in which the boat would be held there. The St. Louis merchant attempted to assist Linnie down the gang-plank, making so much more of the helping than a healthy young woman needed that she pulled away from him in distaste.

She had been hoping he would leave the boat permanently, as he was the only passenger whose presence annoyed her. His persistent seeking of her and his hot breath on her cheek as he bent over her deck-chair filled her with repugnance. Once when she opened the stateroom door, he was sauntering by so slowly and so close to it that she drew back and stayed in all evening. But he was not leaving. Some far-off upriver destination drew him.

It was pleasant to walk again on the solid old earth, the first time since leaving Sioux City, to meet several of the officers' wives and to be the center of interest to them because of her stylish manteau and her butter-bowl hat.

The fort itself looked very rude. Everything in connection with it was so new to Linnie that it kept her brown eyes wide in surprise.

The buildings were placed around a square of ground called the parade, one side of which was occupied by the officers. On two sides were quarters for the soldiers, and on the fourth the hospital and buildings for clothing and commissary stores. Outside of this was a stockade of logs squared and set very close together, with frequent small loopholes for musketry firing, while at opposite corners was a square projection called a bastion. These were two stories high, the lower one containing a swivel-gun which could rake the sides of the wall on occasion, they told her proudly. The upper room was a look-out where a soldier was stationed all day with a powerful field-glass watching for Indians.

A corral was outside but not far away, with a chain of guards on duty day and night on two-hour assignments. It was not pleasant to hear them say this was definitely hostile country and the Indians had been very bad of late. But when they added that the Indians had been more hostile around here than farther up, it lessened her alarm.

Back on the boat the seriousness of her venture confronted her as it had not done before. "I told you not to." "I could come if Mrs. Duncliff could." "But she had reason to." Arguments went back and forth in her disturbed mind as though from two people of opposite nature.

New passengers came on board here, a company of soldiers transferred upstream and the paymaster on his spring trip. He had been on the *Waverly,* which had made such good time it had gone on three days ago.

It took five more days to get to Fort Pierre. The country was definitely wilder and the current becoming swifter. Linnie would not show her disturbed feelings even to Mrs. Duncliff. If she had gone into this too easily and wilfully, the only thing left to do was to put on a brave front and see it through without complaint.

But in another few days she knew the country to

be worse than she had dreamed, nothing but hills of dry sand with little streaks of short shrivel grass in the hollows and on the river bottoms.

Antelope were very numerous now. Several large droves were seen, apparently a hundred or more in each drove. A soldier shot one from the deck, and two members of the crew retrieved it by way of one of the small boats. The next day there were antelope cutlets which every one pronounced of delicious flavor, fine and as tender as a chicken's breast. Not so good the elk meat a few days later. It was tough and strong, and both Linnie and Mrs. Duncliff decided they could do without it very well unless starving.

Sometimes now, just before nightfall, they saw the large gray shadow of a wolf steal down to the river's edge watching—watching—to see the steamboat pass. Sometimes two or three Indians were visible near the water's edge, as silent and as grim as the wolf. They, too, were watching—watching—to see the steamboat pass.

A week out of Fort Randall and the sick Indian woman came out of her room for the first time. She had the distinct features of her race and wore her long black hair in a single braid down her back. It fascinated Linnie, the knowledge that she was a Blackfoot princess. The captain told her that as a young girl the princess had entertained John James Audubon, dressing up for him in her Indian costume, riding for him, fetching him mallard ducks to paint which she had caught by swimming after them in the Missouri. Now at middle age she was influential in maintaining peace between her tribe and the white traders.

A day or two later the captain stopped by to say, "We've passed the last wood yard now and that will slow us up. The crew will have to cut their own fuel whenever we can find it. It's scarce along here for many miles."

The high water had receded, and occasionally a sand-bar shouldered its tawny length ahead of them like the protruding brown shoulder of a drowned giant warrior. High banks on the one side and low banks of sand on the other made a constant change in the channel.

Suddenly, one day, ahead of them was a steam-boat stuck on a sand-bar but fully a quarter of a mile from the present course, so changeable was the river's channel.

It was the *Amelia Poe,* held there since the year before by the wet sands, as though the brown arms of that drowned warrior clutched it and would not let it go. It was disintegrating, sinking slowly into its potter's grave. The captain said the officers of the forts usually purchased and took away the furniture from a stranded vessel for their quarters.

The pilot's wife, standing apart from the group at the deck's railing, said, "The river takes its toll." Her hollow voice sounded like the voice of prophecy.

The country grew wilder and the bluffs higher,

often on both sides of the river now instead of one. The current was swifter too. But the water was low. Twice they had to double trip—unload some of the cargo on the river-bank, then go up some distance where they would unload more, returning for the first and picking up the second on their way upstream again. It all took countless hours, a whole day sometimes for a few miles of progress.

Linnie and her roommate sat on deck, read, sewed, and chatted. In the evening sometimes they even danced a little, as there was a piano on board and a delicate-looking young boy could play. One wondered what so frail a youth could do in this wild country.

Mrs. Duncliff, fountain of information, said that the boats on the lower Missouri carried bands, but she guessed they thought just a piano would be enough away up here.

The dancing made a pleasant change from the monotony of the trip, but it took so much maneuvering to avoid a constant partnership with the merchant that Linnie began making excuses for not participating.

A scene which brought every one on deck one day was the queer formation of stones at the mouth of a river—the Cannonball—truly as round and smooth as the name some one had given it.

The merchant at Linnie's shoulder, his chin almost touching it so that she moved away, said poetically: "Mother Nature's marbles."

The paymaster gave a hearty grunt: "Worn down by ice."

But spring was coming to the north country now in good earnest. Buds of the cottonwoods along the river's banks were bursting into a fine lace. A stunted type of willow was beginning to spill its own green foam into the water's edge. The air was fresh and sweet with the scent of newly washed cedars. Wild ducks flew over. Grouse and plovers and mud hens settled into the shadowy sloughs.

Soon they would be at Fort Rice and Mrs. Duncliff would be leaving. Linnie could not bear to think of the rest of the journey without her, felt a half fear of the prowling fawning merchant when she would not be at her side.

But soon she knew there was more to fear than the fawning merchant. Several of the crew began placing bundles of shingles in double rows around the upper gallery for the protection of the passengers as the boat was entering the region most frequented by hostile Indians. Several times boats of last year had been fired upon from ambush when passing close to the bank.

There was a day, then, of stopping and tying up at the bank for the cutting of wood, since no longer were there any yards available for refueling. All soldiers on board turned in to help the crew in order to shorten the time of staying. The paymaster, fully armed, came to Mrs. Duncliff and Linnie, offering to escort them if the ladies cared to go ashore for the wild flowers plainly visible from the deck. With no invitation to do so the merchant joined them.

They gathered several varieties of spring flowers, some of them unfamiliar to Linnie, but she knew the windflowers and the wood violets and the little lacy ferns as fine as the maiden's hair for which they were named.

Her persistent admirer, coming close, slipped his arm through hers heavily and whispered, "Do you know the language of the flowers? This one is for anticipation."

He had so thoroughly spoiled the simple diversion that she cut short the stroll near the woodcutters and asked Mrs. Duncliff to go back to the boat with her.

They stayed tied to the bank after the woodcutting, for the night was dark and the channel most uncertain. In the early morning Linnie, sleepily realizing that Mrs. Duncliff had dressed and gone on deck, was roused suddenly to wide-eyed alarm by her bursting into the room excitedly.

She was half crying: "Get up . . . Miss Colsworth . . . quick. The pilot's been killed. Indians! They found him just now. Two arrows in him. When the boat was just started . . . pulling away from the shore. He was at the wheel. Oh, I wish I was at the fort with my husband."

Linnie dressed with fingers trembling at the fastenings and went out on deck to find the boat's crew and passengers both in a state of intense alarm.

They took the dead pilot into his quarters. The arrows would have to be cut out of his body, they said. The second pilot took his place. The boat started on.

All day the fright of it hung over the two women. A dozen times they said, "To think we were strolling right around there."

Over on the washstand in drinking mugs were wind-flowers as white as a dead man's face, violets as blue as a dead man's lips.

And all day Linnie took stock of herself. This, then, was what she had come into with no excuse except the obsession that she could not go east without seeing Norman Stafford again and that something larger than the conventions drew her here.

She reviled herself for one who does something too lightly and too thoughtlessly and finds one's self hopelessly entangled with that which is neither slight nor unimportant.

The captain said he would leave the pilot's body for burial at Fort Rice the next day.

Linnie and Mrs. Duncliff went to see the woman. She sat by her husband's body, her weather-beaten face no more solemn than before the tragedy. It was as though she had always known it would happen. And now it was here.

"He's all I have." She kept using the present tense as though he were still living. "He laughs at me when I talk about the danger. I always go back

and forth with him. He's all I have. Back and forth
... back and forth...."

Mrs. Duncliff and Linnie, in their youth, cried all
the tears the older woman could not shed.

Chapter VIII

IT was the middle of the forenoon when they arrived at Fort Rice. To every one's surprise they
found the *Waverly* tied there, although nearly ready
to leave. Evidently the *River Rose* had come
through with less delay, for it had caught up with
the first boat of the season.

Linnie did not leave the deck, merely stood aside
at the guard-rail during the commotion of disembarking. She could see the square enclosure of palisades on a raised point of ground, with blockhouses
on two of the corners, several cabins around it, and
a mixed mass of soldiers and Indians closer at hand
—more Indians, in fact, than she had ever seen at
one time.

A man near-by remarked that they were mostly
from the Yanktonais and Uncpapa tribes and they
were probably looking for their government supplies.

And now that Linnie must say good-by to Mrs.
Duncliff, she found herself loath to see the talkative
little woman leave. The tie formed by the trip had
drawn them together. There was something fright-
ening, too, about being the last woman on the boat.
Even the Indian woman and her white-whiskered

husband and the mischievous young boy were getting off. They lived on up farther, even beyond Fort Berthold, but for some reason they were stopping here.

"Good-by. I'll never forget you, Miss Colsworth."

"Nor I you, Mrs. Duncliff."

"You never *did* tell me if it was as high as a colonel's wife you would visit."

"It's a secret . . . don't tell . . . but it's General Grant."

And they both laughed at the foolish talk. But not for long.

The gang-plank was down and the body of the dead pilot was being taken ashore, the crowd at the guard-rails standing silent and bare-headed.

The wife came up to the two women just before she left.

"I thank you kindly for comin' to sit with me." Her voice held no emotion in its dry twang. She stood for a moment and then added: "I don't need to go back and forth no more." Then she followed the body down the gang-plank.

Behind her walked Mrs. Duncliff, who was soon in the arms of a tall lanky officer. The quick and the dead! What quirk of Fate had given life to one husband and death to the other?

In a short time the *River Rose* was on its way. As Linnie turned from the guard-rails she saw the merchant bearing down upon her with his oily smile, so she went at once to the stateroom. Even without his unwelcome presence, she had no heart or courage to stay out on deck watching the light play on the water and drinking in that sharp smell of the rain-washed land. She could think only of the stark tragedy in that woman's homely weatherbeaten face. Fear, too, which she had not known during the first part of the journey, continually haunted her. For a long time she lay in her bunk, her head in the crook of an arm, trying to fit together the pieces in the puzzles of life, wondering, as she had a hundred times, at her own bold decision.

There was a knock on the door, and when she answered it the clerk of the boat stood there with two letters in his hand. "Are you the same as Miss Cynthia Colsworth?"

Without answering specifically, she asked: "What is it?"

"These two letters were found . . ."

"Oh, yes." She held out her hand and he placed them in it without further questioning.

"One of the crew found a gunnysack of mail on the bank yesterday when they were finishing cutting wood. We went through it this morning."

"But how could a mail sack be there?"

"The captain thinks the officers at Fort Berthold probably hired an Indian runner to bring mail down the river to the fort. He either got tired of his bargain and threw the sack away or was attacked by the Sioux and killed."

The letters for which Cynthia would not wait and for the lack of which she could not be forgiving.

She put them in her bag unopened and sat down on the edge of her bunk. What might have taken place in those months since these letters were written? What if something had happened to Norman Stafford? The long gaunt face of that woman haunted her, and the way she kept saying, "He's all I have!"

A day and another went by, and a week, with the boat tying up each night and armed soldiers and crew members on guard, with the call of the loon and the howl of the coyote in the distance. And always the fear of that moccasined footfall which made no sound.

The sweep of the country was broad and vast. The wilful Missouri ran nearly east now. Willows, brush, tall timber grew on the deposits made in former days by the careless wild ways of its spring waters. In the bottoms of ravines opening into the river, green bushes clung to the earth. Sometimes there were low hills of claylike soil. But always on both banks, high or low, there was nothing but vast space and deep solitude.

It was May now, and spring had followed the *River Rose* up to the north country. On one of the warmer days they suddenly sighted a huge herd of buffalo ahead of them swimming the river in a slant-wise crossing. The boat was ordered pulled to shore while the shaggy creatures went by. A deck-hand, hurriedly making a lasso, snared a half-grown calf, and there was a fine dinner of the fresh meat, very nice and mild, not at all the strong flavor Linnie had expected. The captain spent so much of the meal, however, telling her about buffalo hunts, the Indian ceremony when the buffalo dances were performed over the sick and the fate of the old cayaks, and altogether giving the buffalo meat before her such a definite personality, that she had a mild sensation of cannibalism.

The second Sunday in May was sunshiny but, oddly enough, a sultry day! Unusual for that country and a weather-breeder, the captain called it. He came down deck and dropped into a chair near where Linnie was pretending to read but with little thought of her book.

"Well, Miss Colsworth, I think we'll reach Fort Berthold by night. I hope you'll find your young army man all right. I know there's a young man or you wouldn't have made the long journey. I'm getting old, and I've seen lots of people up and down the river. I wanted to say to you . . . we can't always tell how things will be when we take these first trips in the spring. But everything's all right up there, I guess. Injuns don't attack much in winter. And they've a healthy respect for a well-garrisoned fort and those long iron devils that spit fire." He chuckled. "So I reckon your young officer's all right."

He rose and added with a friendly wink: "And he'll be right on hand waiting for you, for the pay-

master left us and got on to the *Waverly* at Fort
Rice. He'll pass the word along that Miss Colsworth
is right behind him on the *River Rose*."

Norman would think it was Cynthia. How cruel!

But they did not make it by night, for the late
afternoon sent a storm after those unusual sultry
hours. So they tied up within very sight of the fort,
across a bend in the river but in reality several miles
away.

All evening the wind lashed and the rains fell.
Large branches and even whole trees came floating
down the river, so that those last miles would have
been precarious journeying. But it was not the storm
which kept Linnie awake.

After a night in which only fitful sleeping came,
she dressed with nervous haste and went out on the
fore deck as soon as they started at daylight.

Fort Berthold! High above the water on great
banks cut out by the river's flow, she could see it.
The sun came up. The boat was near enough for her
to hear the bugle sound reveille. She could faintly see
the flag go to the top of the flagstaff. Away up here,
even, the flag was floating with all its stars. And now
there would be a new star. Nebraska—the thirty-
seventh! Maybe even Dakota Territory would make
another star some day. The war was over. The
country was still a unit. All that anxiety about it
going to pieces was a thing of the past. There was
just one country. There was just one flag. Away up
here this territory was as much a part of the whole

as New York or Massachusetts. The flag could float here just as rightfully as over the capitol in Washington. But it had been a close call. The nation must never again come so near to falling apart.

All these thoughts were fleeting and not quite complete or orderly, but never in a long life, as her diary indicates, did she cease to remember her arrival in that far-off wilderness just at the thrilling moment of the stars and stripes going up at reveille.

And then there were other things which took her mind, for after weeks without mishap steam-engine trouble developed, and until afternoon they were compelled to wait for the journey's ending. Strangely enough the delay gave her time to bolster her slipping courage. Granted it had been a wild adventure and for a fantastic reason. No matter! Now that it was over she would always have the satisfaction of knowing she had taken it.

She would tell Norman about Cynthia and go back on the next boat. The down journey sometimes was made in one-fifth of the time, the captain had said.

They were docking now. The scene was one of a confused mass of small barges and flatboats at the water's edge, milling soldiers, blanketed Indians, rough-looking ponies, yapping dogs. There was noise and commotion. Two cabin-boys took her satchels and hat-boxes. Every one was surging down the gang-plank, even the men who were going on farther, taking the opportunity as always to stretch their legs on land.

Purposely she stayed back in a sheltered spot on deck, wanting to be the last to leave, partly for Norman's sake and partly for gaining complete possession of herself before the interview. When the crowd had thinned, she stepped out, then back again in a moment of agitation now that the time had come and her late courage seemed oozing.

Then she saw him come swinging up the gangplank and toward her. The sight of him and what she would have to explain filled her with mingled excitement and dismay.

She saw his sudden surprise, heard his astonished *"Linnie!"* and noted the swift look across her shoulder and beyond.

"Where is she?"

A flashing memory came to her of that day he arrived so breathlessly to see Cynthia. Just as then, he would have to know she was not here.

"She didn't come."

"What's happened?"

Even then she sensed that he was thinking only of some temporary delay.

"Norman . . . she's married."

She saw the eagerness wiped from his face and stupid confusion take its place for a brief moment. Then he grinned and started to brush past her. "You're teasing. She's hiding."

"No. She *is* married . . . to George Hemming."

He stopped then and stared at her. "She couldn't..."

"Yes. It's true. She hadn't heard from you for a long time. She didn't know ... how things were with you. George had to go to Chicago ... and so ... they surprised every one...." It all sounded so hollow, so insufficient, so thoroughly inexcusable to tell to this loyal man way up here waiting for the girl he loved. But she went on, out of sheer nervousness and pity: "She was thrown in his company quite a good deal ... she really couldn't ..."

"Stop." He broke in brusquely: "I don't want to hear ... if it's ..." That "if" seemed to give him new hope, and he said darkly: "You're telling me the truth?"

She flushed at that and made no answer.

For long moments he stood, silent and grim. She could see his strained mouth and the play of taut muscles in his face.

"She's the only girl..."

For another tense moment he stood, tried to say, "As long as I live ..." and broke off as though the putting of it into words were impossible.

Then he stiffened his shoulders and swung away from her, apparently wanting to put an end to the tragic interview. Suddenly he turned back.

"What did *you* come up here for?" There was only distaste in his voice that she was not Cynthia.

"I had a feeling I could break it to you easier than write it. Cynthia wanted me to ... to be the one. She's tender-hearted...in a way. I thought I could tell you some of the circumstances...that would put it in a better light. And I had the passage papers she wasn't using." Every reason except that vague one about being pulled up here like the tides to the moon.

"Do you think anything you could *say* would make it any better?"

Suddenly it seemed the most presumptuous thing in the world.

"I did think so. I see now it isn't easier. But there was the paid passage, you know. You remember the passage papers?" She was trying to save her pride. "And I was coming up to Sioux City anyway."

"Sioux City! Why, that's barely a start."

"Yes, I didn't...didn't dream it was so far."

The necessity for coming which had clothed her like a garment fell away, and she might have been standing before him naked and ashamed. It was only a brazen adventure now, without rhyme or reason.

He stood looking down at her, still not quite sensing the stupid thing she had done in a world which was crashing about him. For the second time he swung on his heel and started away. And for the second time he turned back.

"What are you going to do?"

"I thought I'd get off and stay until the next boat comes down." She tried to laugh away a little of the moment's grimness by adding: "All that goes up must come down."

But there was no answering ready grin from him now. "Stay! There's no place *to* stay."

"But there must be."

"Do you think there's a town here with boarding-houses like Omaha? And there are no women here at all ... not even a soldier's wife ... not even the usual laundress and cook." He was looking at her in exasperation. "Why did you do such a foolhardy thing?"

"Then I'll just stay with the boat ... go on up and come back on it."

"Into more dangerous territory? The only woman on board? At least the Indians around here are temporarily friendly."

How could she ever have admired him so deeply, this angered person who was making her feel shame-less and ignorant.

"I'd be all right on the boat, wouldn't I?"

"There's no guarantee. It will have to tie up every night in shallow water. And it'll be gone for weeks."

When she made no comment he went on harshly: "Do you know how Indians treat a white woman captive? No, you wouldn't know, of course. Well, I'll tell you ... so horribly that you would kill your-self before you'd be taken ... and no mercy from the squaws either ... they're worse than the bucks."

At last it had penetrated. For the first time in her sheltered life she had the feeling of fright and for-lornness which comes at the thought of no roof and

no hold on anything natural or substantial. The un-
welcoming fort up above her! The mêlée on shore!
Danger farther up the river! The safe old world
had dropped from under her. No, that was not true.
She herself had kicked the safe old world from
under her.

"I shouldn't have come."

"Of course you shouldn't have come." He said it
roughly and with infinite disgust.

Before this she would not have wanted to hurt
him needlessly, but now she did not care. So she
spoke up spiritedly: "But you had intended to bring
Cynthia right into it."

"That was different. She would have been my
wife. The army wives go ..."

He broke off suddenly and walked over to the
guard-rail. For several moments he stood with set
jaw looking toward the mêlée on shore, that confused mass of Indians, soldiers, animals. Then he
swung back with stiffened shoulders, a gesture she
was later to know well.

"There's one thing that could be done."

She was so embarrassed and frightened now that
in trying to cover it and hold to her poise she swung
to the opposite, saying airily: "Push me overboard?"

"Go through with ... a ceremony. The commanding officer has authority. A lieutenant always has two
rooms. It will give you a place to stay."

"You mean ... ?"

"Go through a marriage ceremony. You and I will know it doesn't mean anything but your safety here at the garrison."

"Oh, I couldn't..."

He threw out a hand in exasperation. "It's the only thing I know to do."

"But not...that."

"All right...just as you say. But I'll tell you one thing...you're not going on up the river alone. And it may be weeks before a boat gets down. If there were any officers' wives here it would be easy enough to visit one...but you must know I can't take you to my quarters." And when she stood, flushed and staring at him, he added crossly, "Well ...if I could...would you want the whole garrison going around winking about you behind your back?"

Still she had nothing but a shocked silence to offer.

"When you go down later in the summer you can explain it all to your uncle...and didn't you tell me the one back east was a lawyer, too? Either one would understand it was only for your safety and have it annulled legally for you." He looked away for a moment and added: "My fellow officers have been expecting...a Miss Colsworth."

At this she said hotly: "Oh, I see. You've been jilted...it's to save your pride."

His face darkened. "Don't put any blame on me. You ran your own head into the noose."

Tears of fright and anger were very near the surface, but she would not yield to their weakness.

If his world had crashed, so had her own—a world of the sixties in which love and marriage were lace-bound valentines, with ardent wooing, maidenly reluctance, and blissful endings.

"I've thought of marriage . . . but not . . ."

"You can still think about it."

"But . . . I never meant anything in my life . . . to be like this."

"Neither did I," he said shortly. "Come on."

Two fiery blood spots on her cheeks, she went slowly ahead of him down the gang-plank, past a disorderly array of baggage, canned goods, and freight boxes, into the milling mass of soldiers, ponies, Indians, and yapping dogs.

Her trunk and satchels were being piled into a two-wheeled cart, with Indian children swarming over them, examining and laughing at the colored flowers on all the hat-boxes.

A thick-set, red-faced officer with pock-marked face came toward them through the noisy crowd.

"Major Halligan," Norman saluted. "I have the great pleasure of presenting you to . . . Miss Colsworth."

"M-i-s-s Colsworth!" The major bent in a stiff and soldierly bow, speaking with thick brogue. "The pleasure is all mine, I can assure you."

"I thank you heartily, Major Halligan."

Then, the formalities of the times over, he took her hand and patted it in informal and fatherly fashion.

"You are just as pretty as I thought ... a darker-eyed and darker-haired colleen than I was alookin' for maybe ... oh, I've seen your pichure, you know ... but even prettier. Let a rough-and-tumble old army man welcome you to your new home."

Chapter IX

THIS was the way, then, in which Linnie Colsworth in the late eighteen-sixties went through
a marriage ceremony with Lieutenant Norman Stafford who loved Cynthia Colsworth her cousin.
There had been no wooing at all. There had been
not one moment of courtship dear to femininity,
and so no romantic betrothal.

And now no gay wedding, this. Just the briefest
kind of ceremony by the flustered commanding
officer, who had never been called upon to perform
such a task before. Nothing he had done at Gettys-
burg half equaled it for perspiring fright.

It took place in the ill-ventilated outer room of
the military post, which had once been a fur-trading
establishment and in which some Indian trinkets, a
stuffed Rocky Mountain sheep, a black-tailed deer,
three prairie chickens, and a pheasant still held
glassy-eyed and musty-odorous watch over the com-
ings and goings of any one having business here.

A Sergeant Smith and the army doctor as the two
witnesses made up the wedding party, all unaware
that the ceremony cloaked anything but the deepest
love. Indeed, tears of sentiment filled the pale blue

eyes of that hard-boiled old bachelor, Sergeant Smith, at the sight of this fresh young woman who had journeyed so far to meet her lover.

The army doctor's eyes held no watery tenderness. He had possessed three wives at various times in his life and all had given him trouble, and here was this smart young lieutenant who didn't know calamity when he saw it.

But to that young lieutenant this short ceremony seemed the best solution to the unforeseen and impossible situation.

It was over now. Let the future take care of itself. Enough that Linnie had temporary protection. Enough for the present that she was fairly safe in the garrison, and behind her back there need be no tongues in the cheeks of two hundred men while she stayed as Lieutenant Stafford's guest in his quarters during these waiting weeks.

The gods must have made merry over the little people who thought they were moving about at their own volition.

After the ceremony, the bride, who was no bride at all, ate supper at the officers' mess, which included only the three, Major Halligan, Lieutenant Stafford, and the doctor.

Then she went with Norman to his quarters, the two rooms which Uncle Sam graciously allowed his lieutenants to occupy.

Probably, in a long and full life, Linnie Colsworth never knew such turmoil of thought and distress of feeling as she did when she walked past Norman Stafford holding open the door to those rooms.

The one into which she stepped was the main or sitting-room. Rather to her surprise it looked quite tasteful and habitable. It was carpeted. It contained a center-table, two rockers, and two straight chairs, a writing-desk and shelf of books, an army cot serving as a sofa and covered with buffalo robes decorated on the flesh side with bright Indian colors.

Norman crossed the room and opened the other door for her, without speaking.

Cynthia's room! It was trying very hard to be charming. But not even the elk skins could cover fully the irregularity of whitewashed walls. However, some one had labored here very lovingly. And quite suddenly and for the first time since arriving, she felt as sorry for Norman as for herself.

This room, too, was carpeted. There was a deerskin across the foot of the bed. Beaver skins were thrown down to form small soft rugs. There was a water pitcher on a walnut stand with bowl and towels. A little dressing-table, made from boxes, with gay calico tacked on for curtains, stood under a walnut-framed mirror. The table held candles in odd horn holders, a glass coal-oil lamp and shell-covered handkerchief box. Cynthia, smiling, was looking out at the two from an opened white-carved case. Cynthia had reason to smile.

Two soldiers brought Linnie's baggage, the big trunk and the two large satchels and the three color-spangled hat-boxes, so that the room was filled with them.

Norman pulled aside a calico curtain and took from behind it armfuls of his clothes which he hung back of another curtain in the sitting-room, returning for a bootjack and a shaving kit.

When Linnie stood, unmoving and uncertain, surveying the heaped-up baggage in her room, he came back to the door.

"Why don't you sit out here? I'll be gone for a while."

"I thank you ... I'll sit a little while ... and then unpack a few of my things ... the—the ones I'll need for just a short time." He must be reminded that she could be getting out of his way soon.

When he was ready to leave the quarters, he stopped and turned at the outside door, hesitating over what he was to say.

"I hope you won't be too upset. It was the best thing to do under the circumstances."

At the faint touch of sympathy in his voice, Linnie bit her lips to intercept their quivering. "I'm ... so humiliated," she managed to say. "I didn't think ..."

"Don't worry. Everything has been pretty much of a mistake."

"There were the passage papers...." Like the raven to its "nevermore," she was going back to that weak reason.

"When a boat comes down and you get ready to

go back ... we can talk it over. One of your uncles will take care of everything for you. I'm sure you can make either one understand the situation. In the meantime, make yourself comfortable. And take your time about going over to breakfast. I'll speak to the cook."

The moment the door closed she could not get into the privacy of her room—Cynthia's room—fast enough to bolt the door and throw herself on the bed and shed wild bitter tears for the anger and mortification that filled her. And for something else which was lost and would never return.

After a time when her emotion had spent itself she undressed and lay under the coarse army blankets and the deerskin. Later she heard him come in and move about the sitting-room. For an hour or more the light shone under her door. Then it went out, and all was still except for the howling of animals—coyotes or dogs, she could not tell which—and the lone sad cry of a loon. So unbelievable was this fantastic situation in which she found herself, so active her mind in going over the whole wild happening from its beginning, that she knew she could never sleep again. But nature must have played a trick on her, for the next thing her startled senses knew she was sitting up in bed.

"What are those sounds?" At first she thought she had said it aloud, but realized at once it had been only in her dreaming.

They were bugle notes, sounding reveille. And some one was stirring about in the other room.

When the outer door closed after a time, she rose to dress. It was evidently river water in the big china pitcher, for there was a murkiness all through it and she had to pour it carefully so as not to thicken it with the silt at the bottom. When she had finished washing, she looked into the little walnut glass to see whether she was more or less clean. Then she dressed, choosing one of her wide-skirted morning prints, a blue flower on a tan background, and tying a blue ribbon around her head in line with her dark braids.

Even though there was no sound in the sitting-room, she opened the door a mere crack and peeped cautiously through before venturing out. Not only was he gone, but he had made up his army cot and put his things out of sight so that the room looked as neat as it had the previous evening.

Then she stepped out and went at once to the officers' mess as he had told her to do.

A young soldier, evidently assigned to this task, came immediately to bring her a breakfast of flapjacks, dark molasses, and coffee, the alacrity with which he brought it giving ample proof that the cakes had been around for some time awaiting her arrival. He made her rather nervous, though, for so deeply solicitous was he of her welfare that he practically watched her every bite disappear.

When she had eaten sparingly of the cakes, so

truthfully called "flannel," she thanked the youth with a smile which must have upset him, as he instantly dropped the molasses jug, but retrieved it deftly before the slow-moving syrup could escape.

Apparently she was her own entertainment committee, so strolled about until she came to a stairway. Peering up cautiously, she climbed the stairs to a lookout in which, to her surprise, there was no guard as in the one at Fort Randall. So for a time she stood by herself, taking in the sights below and before her.

The location of the fort was a happy one there on the high river-bank. The Missouri, on which she had spent so many weeks, was visible for a long distance, sparkling this morning in the sunshine like a gipsy, a Romany who is gay in a bright-colored shawl which covers a dirty body. And the country beyond looked very rough and wild.

Immediately below her was a wide dry ditch, but for what reason she did not know.

However, it was the Indian village which held her interest. Looking down upon it she could see that there was neither plan nor arrangement for it. There were no streets or symmetrical placing of tepees, just a conglomerate mass of hundreds of huts with rounded domes as though they had been dropped from a height and had landed anywhere. There was activity all about in its confines, every age of Indian coming and going in the winding paths between the dwellings.

For some time she stood gazing at the scene try-ing to believe she was really looking at it and not dreaming, when she heard a step behind her. She turned in quick alarm to see Norman coming in.

He was not the trimly uniformed lieutenant of last evening but was dressed in his field-service uni-form with loose tunic. Plainly he had been working or riding, for he was neither trim nor immaculate.

"Here you are," he spoke shortly. "Didn't think you'd be so foolish as to walk out by yourself."

"No, I wouldn't." She was desperately ill at ease but made special effort not to let him see it. "I'd not feel safe with all those Indians."

"You'd be safe enough, but they would probably annoy you." He was standing by her now looking down into the village, his manner polite and aloof. "They have the curiosity of children."

"Then they're not dangerous?"

"That's hard to answer. They're friendly enough right now. They always cuddle up to the army when they want security, and just now they're here for protection from their enemy, the Sioux. Last fall they were running amuck."

"What is this tribe?"

"There are three. Each has its own section of the village. They're the Mandan, the Arikara, and the Gros Ventres. That last means Big Bellies, if you want a translation."

It was strong language for a delicate young lady of the times, and he must have known it.

"And there's a chief?" she asked hurriedly.

"Three, of course: Crow Belly, Red Cow, and White Shield."

"The other two sound mean. But White Shield! he sounds like a nice gentleman."

His mouth drew down at the corners for a fleeting moment in the way she remembered so well. "Your nice gentleman allowed one of his enemies to be cut up in little pieces last fall," he said dryly.

She had to shudder at that but suddenly felt less uncomfortable in his presence.

"There are no other white people here besides the soldiers?"

"A few French fur traders who have been here a long time and have Indian wives and families. One or two have families back home, too," he added frankly.

"How disgusting!"

"Oh, you can't blame them. They're lonely, and a union like that gives them an advantage with the tribe."

Plainly this was no female seminary atmosphere up here in the Indian country.

Suddenly he turned to her with: "Did you rest?"

"Yes, I thank you," she lied politely.

"Dogs didn't keep you awake?"

"Only a little."

"No bedbugs?"

This time she was genuinely shocked, for no one

ever said the words out loud. "Good gracious, no. Are there . . . ? Do you . . . ?"

"Then my days of labor with a chicken feather and coal-oil were not in vain." He dismissed the subject as trivial and took up another. "Would you like to go out and walk through the village for a closer view?"

So she went back to the quarters for her new sunbonnet, but changed her mind suddenly and got out a more becoming wide-brimmed garden hat with ribbons on it.

They went through the sallyport and on out to the village. As they walked along, a few women and children ran in front of them peering up into Linnie's face, which was somewhat shaded by her big hat. These were joined by others and others, the new-comers always taking their turn to peer up into the white woman's face, until the crowd might have numbered almost a hundred. Each time the late arrivals joined the cavalcade they would fall back with a great deal of laughing and chattering.

When Norman saw that she was irritated and half-frightened, he sought to put her at ease with: "Well, you would want to see the foreign animals at the circus, wouldn't you?"

But the fear of the strange brown people was instinctive, and she could not throw it off. Nor could she do so all the years of her life. As long as she lived she could not conquer that tenseness of nerves in the presence of the mildest one of the race.

Their walk took them past a tepee where two Indian women were preparing a buffalo robe for use. It was stretched and pinned to the ground and had been scraped free from fat, so that now they were rubbing and pounding it. They looked up in wonderment at Linnie for a few moments and then went stolidly on with their work. Evidently here were two old women who were minding their own business.

Norman made known by signs, pointing to Linnie's feet and to the red handkerchief knotted about his neck, that he would trade for moccasins. So one ambled into the tepee like a fat old buffalo and returned with a fine, intricately beaded pair which she traded without the flicker of an eyelid for the cheap bandana.

Linnie was pleased with her gift and took pains to let him know it.

They came in time to the tepee of one of the white traders living there with his squaw wife and halfbreed children. He invited them in and visited with them in laborious English with an occasional French word, but the woman in soiled calico said "How," and nothing more.

There was a fire in the middle of the tepee under the smoke-hole, and great piles of buffalo, beaver and deer skins were piled in confusion.

The children, either from an innate sense of the proprieties or from timidity, stayed back in the shadows, and only occasionally was there the glimpse of a bare copper-colored body flitting from one bundle of skins to another.

As guest of honor, Linnie was given the cracker-box seat covered with a beautiful beaver skin. A large kettle, evidently containing the cooking dinner, was hanging over the fire, for the trader told them hospitably if they would stay a while it would be ready to eat.

She glanced in horror at Norman and found him looking quizzically at her, the merest suggestion of a twinkle in his eye, as he gravely thanked his host and explained they were expected back at mess time.

So they strolled back through the sallyport, these two human beings who thought they were handling their own lives as deliberately as one moves wooden chessmen about.

At the door of their quarters Norman stopped to say: "Then we'll make the best of it—shall we—while you're here?"

"Yes. And now there's something I have wanted to tell you. I have two of your letters."

She went into her own room and returned with the unopened messages.

He stared at them in mystification.

"Where did you get them?"

"One of the crew found them in a sack when we tied up for wood, probably a day's journey the other side of Fort Rice."

He stood looking at them with deep repugnance

as though they were alive, two erstwhile friends who had betrayed him.

She saw the muscles in his lean face grow tense, and knew instinctively what he was thinking: that if they had reached their destination Cynthia would have come.

But Linnie knew better. She knew now that Cynthia never would have come at all.

And now all the easy companionship of the morning had vanished. Silently he put the letters in his desk and left.

Chapter X

ON the second afternoon of this queer arrangement for living, Norman came to the quarters to ask if Linnie would like to come to the mess-room and attend a pow-wow.

"Oh ... what do I wear ... and how do I act?" she asked apprehensively.

"Your best white doeskin with the porcupine quills," he answered, jocularly, "and just act dumb like a squaw."

It was a touch of his friendly self in contrast to those moments when he had been miles away in thought, not only preoccupied but gruff.

When she entered the mess-room with him, the three chiefs, White Shield, Crow Belly, and Red Cow, were seated on the floor with backs against the wall. Major Halligan seemed to call their attention to her. To her surprise and consternation, each one in turn rose, crossed the room, shook hands with her, and uttered his "How." Suddenly she turned cold and a little sick to see that one had two long-haired scalps at his belt.

Viewed without prejudice, they were magnificent specimens of masculinity. Sometimes their robes, held only by their hands, slipped down from their splendid shoulders, the muscles playing underneath the smooth brown skin. Their moccasins were pieces of intricate beadwork, their necklaces of beads or bears' claws.

From time to time other warriors came into the room—Poor Wolf, Son-of-the-Star, Long Bone, and Eagle-Who-Hunts-Eagles, Norman told her later.

Coffee was served and the peace-pipe lighted and passed around from one to the other in perfect silence. Then a long grave talk began, the interpreter, a French half-breed, translating in turn for both officers and Indians.

White Shield, the Arikara chief, who spoke first, gave a dignified and almost unending talk about the friendly relations between the Three Tribes and the whites. "We are peaceful. We cultivate the good ground. Our enemies harass us. They kill our young men. They steal our horses."

It ended finally in a request for guns and ammunition that they might more speedily dispose of their enemy.

"You'll be able to give lectures about them when you go back, like these ranting platform women," Norman said when at last they were outside.

And she knew from the tone of his voice how very little he liked the new kind of independent woman —the kind who would take a long river trip alone for the sake of adventure.

The arrangement at the quarters continued to be carried out without difficulty. Norman was up and

away at reveille. All day the rooms were Linnie's
own. They met at the two meals, and with the
major and the doctor present the conversation
stayed general and without intimacy. And Norman
was very busy all day and into the evening. Whether
or not he made extra tasks for himself she had no
way of knowing.

In the later evening she would slip into her room,
where she read or sewed a bit by the light of the stylish glass lamp with its stepped-up base, and with
Cynthia forever smiling enigmatically at her across
the dressing-table. Sometimes she had a deep urge
to put the picture away so that Cynthia could no
longer laugh at this predicament, but she would not
let herself do so.

When Norman was gone, the place became her
own, so she kept it immaculate, even dismissing the
orderly from the hospital who came over to help.

The lieutenant seemed conscientious about doing
something for her entertainment, if such it could
be called when the trips were so limited. So once
a day he would come back to the quarters to get her
for a brief excursion.

"Where shall we go to-day?" he would ask.
"Stroll around Washington Square or do the Bat-
tery?"

It brought them together for the moment, that
knowledge of having been at the same places, having
shared the same experiences. He had a courteous

dignity with her always, as though he would see this thing through faithfully if it killed him.

Once they walked down on the river bottom where the squaws were planting corn. The Indian women would dig a patch of ground and make little holes laboriously, but instead of covering them with their hoes they would stoop down and use their hands, patting the ground as one would pat dough.

"It's a kind of rice corn," he told her. "It will grow about two feet high and have little ears only three or four inches long. It matures in a couple of months. The season is short here and the summer will be over very early."

It made her feel self-conscious, so that she said, "There will be a boat going down soon, surely?"

"It all depends. There would be, if one had tied up for the winter farther up, but my guess now is that none did."

"But what about these out here?"

"Flatboats ... mackinaws ... bull-boats, just used to cross the river or for short trips."

Suddenly he turned to her, and now he was the self-conscious one.

"About that first boat down. You accused me of wanting to save my pride before my fellow-officers. It angered me at the time but maybe there was a bit of truth in it. I find I do have a little about you leaving on the first one. One just isn't a—so-called bride—one day and leaving the next. . . ."

"Oh, but I planned. . . ."

"If you're not terribly uncomfortable ... you could stay until the second boat. You might as well be hung for a sheep as a lamb." He grinned. "Captain Halligan said it kept him shaved and polished to have you here. Even the old pessimist doc grudgingly likes you."

"Oh ... I hadn't ..."

"There may be officers' wives coming down later from Fort Buford or the Montana posts for company. And passage on a late summer boat is cheaper than the earlier ones, too."

She flushed at that. "I have my own money."

"I didn't mean the expense especially. It was just one of the reasons."

So—the diary does not tell why—but when the June boat finally came down she did not take it. Why did the wild geese not fly south in June? Or the snows cover the river hills? Or the moon fail to ride the night skies?

And then four hundred Yankton Sioux arrived to trade dried meat and skins.

The chief, Fool Dog, paid the officers an official visit. He was extremely friendly, probably hoping to get special favors, but in spite of his overtures, which they decided were somewhat overdone, Major Halligan made known to him through the interpreter that he would not be allowed to let his followers enter the fort but must camp on the river bottom some distance away.

He was wonderfully decorated for the occasion.

Besides the regulation dress of buffalo skin and moccasins he wore a row of ornaments attached to the
rims of his ears, which had been perforated for that
purpose and now held an assortment of mussel
shells, elks' teeth and bears' claws. His face was
painted blue with clay from the river-bank, and his
sense of artistry had caused him to scratch it before
it dried so that the lines converged in his eyes, which
were surrounded by owl-like red streaks. But the
last word in his striking get-up had the white man's
touch—bracelets on both wrists made from tin tomato cans with the ends removed but the red pictured paper covering intact.

As the interview was ending, Linnie came to the
door of the mess-room, thinking to peep in upon the
lordly visitor and not be seen. But Fool Dog was
just taking his dignified self away, teeth, claws,
shells, tomato cans, and all.

Linnie looked rather dressed up herself in her
mushroom skirts of flowered green muslin. At any
rate Fool Dog grunted his approval, turned back
and told the interpreter to tell the major and the
lieutenant that he was prepared to give buffalo hides
and beaver skins for her.

When Linnie in fright was slipping away, Norman called to her sharply to stay where she was.
After Fool Dog had gone, he told her never to act
afraid. No matter what the occasion, she must stand
her ground. Then he explained what the chief
wanted, and added with the droll grin which some-

times showed itself of late: "He should have come
around the other day when I didn't know what to do
with you." So that Linnie laughed and felt lighter-
hearted than she had since her arrival.

Sometimes in their walks he told her bits of local
history—how the fort was built as an American Fur
Company post years before, how it had been nearly
captured by the Sioux, had been a military post only
three years. Even now there was surmise that it was
to be abandoned, but the Indians were not to know
that.

"Don't tell your young man friend, Fool Dog,"
he grinned.

And she liked him better for his occasional flashes
of fun in the days of his hurt over Cynthia.

He told her about the trader who, knowing there
was to be an eclipse, informed the Indians he would
hang his hat on the moon that night and in what awe
he was held afterward. About the artist, Rudolph
Kurz, who was in this very place years before when
it was a trading-post—how he sketched and painted
pictures of the Indians, and when a sickness came
on them, they turned upon him, attributing it to the
portraits.

He took her down to show her how he was sending a hayrack across the river by having four
squaws, each in a bull-boat under a wheel, paddle it
across. The bull-boats were queer affairs, made
simply of buffalo hides sewn together in the form

of round tubs and held in shape by wooden frames.

The squaws were laughing their heads off, so Norman and Linnie had to join in, too, realizing that laughter can be an intertribal and international thing.

He took her one evening to see the Indians at a swimming party. They stopped far enough back so that they could neither annoy nor be annoyed. And a gala event it proved to be: brown bodies leaping from a steep bank into the water so thick with human beings that it must have been hard for one to keep from landing on another. Some of the little tots appeared to be only two or three years old, but their elders would pick them up and toss them into the stream as carelessly as though the loss of a few here and there would not matter in the least.

"This is the very crowd," he told her, "that last fall left all their squaws and children here in camp and went out to hunt up their enemy, the Sioux, met up with them and killed one, scalped him and cut him up, and brought the pieces back for a song and dance pow-wow. You wouldn't think it to look at these merry hi-jinks to-night, would you?"

There was the dance by two hundred friendly Indians in the sallyport, with Major Halligan so pessimistic in regard to the constancy of their love and affection for the whites that he took no chances about allowing them in the fort and had a company of soldiers armed and ready for duty at the word of command.

From a vantage point Linnie watched them with Norman.

The affair was the "scalp" or "brave heart" dance in honor of a victory over the enemy, an Uncpapa chief, one of the most hostile of the bands of Sioux.

Some wore buffalo horns and were painted in the manner of overlapping scales. One wore a white horsehair wig with a bright red streak of paint where the hair was parted over the forehead. One had long bears' claws for finger-nails, and by what means they were fastened on was a question which Norman could not answer.

For a long time they watched the circle with its continuous changing of participants, some in the center keeping up their rhythmic time to the sound of several rude drums, soon to be replaced by others.

He took her down to the running races once and to the horse racing another time, asking her if she wanted to go to Saratoga that afternoon.

A day later they went out to the Indian burying-ground where were the aerial tombs of the dead.

On the roundabout way back they saw a group of Indians surrounding some object, and when she grew curious, he slipped an arm about her shoulder and turned her way.

"What was it?"

"Not a pretty sight," he said and dropped his arm. "Those are the torture posts, *self*-torture I mean. They go there to obtain from the Great Spirit their heart's desire . . . a good crop . . . success in the hunt ... somebody's scalp. This was a youth with slits in the skin on his back and a pole through them. When he breaks the skin he will be a grown-up young man and there'll be a great feast. But if he cries out or faints he'll have to work with the women."

It was that night she was awakened by screeching, groaning, and dogs barking, so that she sat up shaking with fright.

Norman tapped on her door. "Awake?"

"Yes."

"Not scared, are you?"

"What ... what ... is it?"

"Only a young warrior serenading his lady love ... but you're not it, so you can go back to sleep."

At the noon meal he told her: "You'll have to live through it several nights. He keeps it up, bringing a new pony each night until the girl's father thinks he's contributed enough. Then she's all his'n."

Major Halligan and the doctor laughed with her at Norman's explanation. It was in moments like this that she felt at home here and seemed to become a part of the life around her, otherwise so new and strange.

Once in the village they met Father De Smet, white-haired and gentle of face, in his late sixties now. He was going back to St. Louis to stay, but the Indians always would be his concern.

Although not of his church, suddenly Linnie wished

that she were able to tell him of this strange thing which had happened to her. In the saintliness of his presence the vows she had spoken without meaning seemed wrong and unjustified. Life was very queer.

And then Norman came in one day with the sequel to the finding of the mail-bag on her journey up-river.

An Indian had come into the post to tell the interpreter that he was a friend of the runner who had been entrusted with the mail-bag last winter. Major Halligan, having many official communications and reports for the States, as well as personal letters, had hired a friendly Indian to take them down to Fort Rice. He had gone only about half the distance when he was captured by a band of hostile Cheyenne Sioux. The mail-bag had been opened and examined by their big medicine man, and was then ordered to be burned. Then a council of war was held to decide what to do with the carrier.

" 'He is a friend of the whites. The whites are our enemies. So he is our enemy' was their argument," Norman told her. "Sort of like, 'Things that are equal to the same thing are equal to each other,' isn't it? But there was more reasoning: 'He must be a very brave man or he would not have dared pass through our country alone. So while we know him to be our enemy we will give him his liberty as a reward for his courage.' The runner was afraid he'd be blamed and didn't come back but sent this

Indian friend. He thought the sack had been burned until I told him about my letters."

Those letters to Cynthia! And now Norman was in one of his quiet moods again, courteous, unsmiling, and very far away.

Chapter XI

THE days had gone into weeks and the weeks into a month. And now the month, too, was going. Sometimes Linnie loathed her surroundings and knew when the next boat came down she would say good-by to them with deepest relief: the dirty river water, those eternal noises of dogs and coyotes, the heavy pancakes and strong coffee, and that Indian-and-buffalo-hide odor which permeated everything and which her nostrils were never to forget to her dying day!

In spite of all this, the life half-fascinated her, too. Reveille and retreat, the sight of the stars and stripes forever whipping up there in the blue, the constant and sometimes colorful movement about her, the casual talk of army life at officers' mess, the freedom from former social obligations—to all these she responded like one to the army born.

She was thinking all this on a warm afternoon as she sat mending one of her flowered prints, when Norman came to the door of the sitting-room.

The moment he came in she knew he had something unusual to tell her. In this brief time she had learned his moods. This was the one in which he snapped to action. She had noticed it in him many times. It was as though constitutionally he might be a slow, listless person, but underneath that languid exterior were fibers of steal.

Now, still standing just inside the door, he said with no preliminaries: "I'm ordered to Camp Cooke."

"Camp Cooke. Where is that?"

"Up in the Montana Territory."

"And ... you're obliged to go?" She sensed at once she was asking a foolish question of an army man.

" 'Orders is orders.' "

"When?"

"First boat upriver."

"Then I'll ... I'll just stay here and take the next boat down."

"It's not so simple as that. Fort's to be abandoned."

"Oh ... I should have gone on that first boat. What shall I do?"

"Looks as though you'd have to go along."

"And if I started ... maybe we would pass a boat going down?"

"I've thought of that ... but I can't just picture you hailing one and piling overboard with that big trunk and all those satchels and boxes."

Even in the gravity of the situation she had to laugh, so that he added facetiously, "I should have traded you to Fool Dog when I had a chance." Then he sobered. "I think if you keep to the original plan

—go on up to Camp Cooke with the company and
take a boat down from there—it will be better all
around."

"To go . . . on up there?"

"Yes. There may even be officers' wives going
out for the winter for company. So pack your duds."

She packed her own things and some of the furnishings of the little bedroom and Cynthia's picture
forever smiling at this awkward dilemma.

There was a great deal of activity around the
post, a dismantling of guns and a packing of ordnance by all hands. A faithful (so far) Indian em-
ployee was to be guardian of the grain left in storage
and to keep the women and children from stealing
it if possible. Major Halligan and the doctor were
ordered to the new Fort Stevenson, which as yet
was a mere collection of tents.

And then Norman came in hurriedly to tell her
the *Luella,* a small stern-wheeler, had just come
upstream. It reported Indian trouble en route two
nights when the boat was tied up. The captain was
much relieved to know he was taking on a company
of soldiers, as he was short-handed for a crew and
he hadn't relished those attempted attacks. The boat
would be loaded to the guard-rails when this company was added.

"The water's low," Norman told her, "but you
know they say a small stern-wheeler can run on a
heavy dew."

A young soldier came with the two-wheeled cart

and took the trunk and the satchels and all the gay
flowered hat-boxes down the steep path to the shore.
That same mêlée confronted her, a conglomerate
mass of ponies, Indians, dogs, soldiers, baggage.

She stood by her own things so that no harm
would come to them while Norman was seeing to
arrangements. Two men near her were talking about
one of the North brothers down in Nebraska having
a battalion of Pawnees under him to protect the
new Union Pacific from the Sioux.

"I'd like to see old Turkey Leg and Tall Bull,"
one of the men near her got out between squirts of
tobacco juice, "when they find them old Pawnee
enemies of their'n 'quipped with good rifles and the
U.S. government ahind 'em."

"Biggest mistake in the world to put a gun in a
Injun's hands."

And then Norman came. "It will be very crowded.
You're to share the stateroom of a lieutenant's wife
traveling alone. She's en route to Camp Cooke, too."

On board after all the noise and excitement, she
found her room-mate to be a Mrs. Lane, a quiet
person, in complete contrast to Mrs. Duncliff, Linnie's talkative cabin-mate from Omaha to Fort Rice.
The young woman was not very well or was at least
in a state of mental distress, as she lay on her bed a
great deal. In the late afternoon when Linnie found
her in tears she asked if there was anything she
could do.

"No." The young Mrs. Lane broke into fresh sobbing. "You can't do anything for homesickness."

Questioning her, Linnie found that the young woman had been living with her parents in St. Louis and had grown so homesick for her husband that she was on her way to join him. But now that she was here in this wild country, she was not sure she should have come. Apparently, life was bearing down upon her heavily like a smothering blanket, and she had no courage to sit up and throw it off.

The only other women were two blowsy-looking creatures who talked loudly about the gold mines and Virginia City, and as Linnie did not like their looks, she usually busied herself on deck with a book or bit of sewing. Sometimes Norman came to sit with her and, like two old friends, they conversed about the various interests along the way.

For there was a great deal to hold their attention. In time the way became harder, the scenery bolder and grander. Sometimes they seemed to be headed straight for the bluffs, only to find that they were entering a sharp bend in the river. Every day there was some special animal life to see: a drove of buffalo, elk, or antelope. Once when the current of the stream took them close to shore, Linnie thought she saw a grotesque animal in a tree. She called Norman to come and look at it, but he said it was only a dead Injun sewed into a buffalo skin.

Every day as they went on upstream, the bluffs

grew steeper and the Missouri River mountains became visible. And every night they tied up where the
water was low and the current swift. Two of the
crew kept the boiler fires stoked so that no time
would be lost if Indians attacked, and they could
push out into the stream immediately. And guards
sat fore and aft all night.

One day when they stopped to cut wood, crew,
soldiers, and officers alike turned in to work so that
the time for staying would be shortened.

It seemed good to be on land again, and Linnie
walked briskly about, and then, attracted by the possibility of the view from the bluffs, started up the
nearest one, only to hear Norman call sharply:
"Linnie! Come back here."

It embarrassed her before the big crowd of men.
And when she saw the two blowsy women laughing
with some of the crew about it, she went back to
the boat's deck as chagrined as a child who had been
punished before company.

The next day was the Fourth of July, and although there was no stopping of the slow-moving
boat or any of the crew's activities, the passengers
gathered in the little cabin for a short patriotic
meeting. As he had said nothing about it, Linnie
was surprised when Norman took charge.

There were some patriotic songs and then Norman himself gave a brief talk, saying no matter
where in the nation one was stationed, whether in
the midst of activities in the capital, or in eastern

city life or western village, in the farthest trading-post or the most outlying of the frontier forts, there lay one's faithful duty to one's country. That the country needed the army's services out here to bring law and order to it. But that the army was dependent upon other people back in the States to accomplish it, so that it was clear no man lived for himself. This western country had a great future. The day might come when here in the Dakota and Montana territories there would be many settlers and law and order, schools and churches and good homes. In some far-distant day the Indians themselves might be peaceful and law abiding.

Linnie found herself quite thrilled over his talk and very proud of him, putting out of her mind those insistent questions about her future as one closes a book apprehensively, fearful to read on lest one may not like the ending.

Five days later they stopped at Fort Buford where two officers and their wives came on to the boat for a short time, saying it was pleasant to meet and talk with outsiders.

The women said it had been nearly a year since they had seen any other white women. They examined the way Linnie's dress and manteau were made and asked her if she had scissors handy so that they might cut a pattern of her wrist-bag.

Hostile Indians had stayed near Fort Buford so constantly during the past year that the women had never been able to leave the palisades, except for a few times when, desperate to get outside, they had accompanied the armed men going to the river to fill the water casks.

Linnie marveled at them, wondering how they could be anything but insane, to say nothing of interested in the cut of a manteau and wrist-bag.

Fort Union was such a short distance away that a few of the soldiers got permission to walk across land and join the boat there.

And now they were in Montana territory, for they passed the Yellowstone River, so turbid and yellow that they could easily follow its current as it poured into the Missouri, which, strangely enough, differing from its quality down in Nebraska, was clear over a rocky sandy bottom. The largest herd of buffalo they had seen swam the river ahead of them, a shaggy old bull at the head, looking defiant in his contempt and so heavy that one wondered he could swim at all.

They passed Fort Peck. It was only a fur trading-post, but strongly fortified. When the Crows came in to trade, some one explained, the gates were shut and all business was conducted through a small opening in the wall which could be closed at a moment's notice.

Two days later Bird Rapids confronted them— a shoal of rock across the river over which the water came dashing and foaming, seeming inpassable to inexperienced eyes. But the captain sent a hawser above the rapids, made it fast to a large tree, and by the use of the queer capstan took them safely over.

The river still stayed beautifully clear with many small streams flowing into it—the Milk, the Musselshell, and others.

They were nearly at their journey's end now, and the face of the country was bare except in the river valleys, where there was grass and cottonwood timber and on the mountains masses of stunted cedars. Bunch grass, like cured hay, and sage-brush, those dwarfed and hoary old men of the alkali plains, were the only visible vegetation.

Sitting on deck while the little stern-wheeler puffed up the narrowing stream, looking at the mountains, the cedars, the sage-brush, Linnie would close her eyes and say to herself: "It isn't so. I'm not here. I'm on the front stoop with Uncle David and Aunt Margaret. I'm in the back parlor with Uncle Henry and Aunt Louise and Cynthia. I, Linnie Colsworth, didn't do that wild, foolhardy, adventuresome thing." Then she would open her eyes to mountains, cedars, sage-brush, and the deck of a little steamer.

It was late forenoon when they arrived at Camp Cooke. They found the fort built in design like the other, with bastions, stockades, and moat. But as considerable timber grew on the river bottoms there was a sawmill, and the rows of houses were framed of wood and filled in with adobe bricks, something very new to the eastern girl. Also new to her were the roofs of the houses made of poles laid at intervals and coming to a peak in the center with brush and earth packed over them. These various units for officers joined each other, and a long porch in front was common to all.

The fort was on the south side of the Missouri, where the Judith flows into the river, the Missouri lying north and the Judith east. To the west and south they were surrounded by the foothills of the mountains with their ranges in the distance, while across the river, north, like an artist's oil painting of immense size and indescribable grandeur was a view of the Bears Paw Mountains, seemingly isolated peaks on a comparatively level stretch of country and perhaps thirty miles away.

There was much confusion, as their arrival made seven companies in all for the moment, until the two ordered on to headquarters at Fort Shaw were started off on the *Luella* and another waiting stern-wheeler, the *Maybelle*.

Norman was assigned to the four-room unit just vacated by an officer and his wife. There was no officers' mess as at Fort Berthold, and the commanding officers' wife invited them to eat until such time as they could get settled.

Linnie liked her at once. It was pleasant to be with women again, and this Mrs. Talcott was middle-aged and motherly with a sense of humor which often sent her small fat body into shaking chuckles. She had a single child, a son at West Point, to whom she referred often and proudly. The colonel was tall and gray and grizzled, a quiet man who read constantly in his leisure moments and in conversation bit off his words as though they were gingersnaps.

Mrs. Talcott said she would get Linnie a servant from the soldiers' wives, of which there were six here. But Linnie said not to bother because she was going out now very soon.

"You are!" The Colonel's wife looked at her with tolerant surprise. "I guess I'm the old-fashioned kind of army wife. Maybe the colonel rather I *would* go...." Her body shook with laughter. "But I just stick like a fat leech. The colonel says I can be satisfied anywhere if I have a cracker-box to put a table-cloth on and a spot to hang up 'God Bless Our Home.'"

When they were back at the new quarters, Norman said: "Did you mean that about no servant? Can you cook?"

"What...at Camp Cooke?" she asked him. And they both laughed.

It was only an hour later that he came back to the quarters with the nearest approach to excitement which Linnie ever had seen in him.

"You know Mr. Robinson Crusoe? Well, there's everything on this particular island, too, excepting the man, Friday. Lieutenant Lane's just come in with the news that a steamer on a near-by bar is breaking up. They've given up trying to get it off and

are ready to sell the furnishings. Some of the officers
are going in flatboats and get them."

"Oh ... not on my account," Linnie protested.
"I'm going back down in so short a time...."

"Who said anything about you?" he wanted to
know.

It was the height of excitement for the various
wives, that return of the braves from their conquest.
Norman had furniture, dishes, enough ingrain carpet for two of the rooms, and as his special pride
and joy, a huge gilt-framed mirror reaching from
floor to ceiling of the main room, taken from the
bar of the steamer, and with a golden mermaid at
the top.

"She's fly-specked." Norman said, "She needs
scrubbing."

She needs more than scrubbing, Linnie thought
to herself, because of the scantiness of draperies, but
did not say it.

After a few days of hard work the newly fur-
nished rooms were rather splendid, at least for army
quarters.

From her vantage point in the steamer's bar, the
golden mermaid must have seen strange sights but
probably none more strange than she now looked
down upon, two mature people playing a childish
game.

Chapter XII

For the first time Linnie witnessed dress parade with all officers and men in full uniform. She found herself thrilling to bugles and banners and marching men, that showy frame-work of the old Indian-fighting army which at times held the vision away from the real picture, allowing one to forget the dangers and the deaths.

There were four officers' wives besides Linnie—who was no wife at all, only a guest. But that no one knew.

There was the colonel's wife, Mrs. Talcott, with her little fat body, her full-moon face and easy laughter.

Mrs. Norris, the captain's wife, was the mother of two girls and a boy, a harassed woman who was in a perpetual state of worry over her offspring, their lack of educational advantages, their boisterous activities, their democratic associations with tough old sergeants and tough young orderlies. The children were Effie, Essie, and Ezra, and sometimes, in their boyish clothes and hoyden-like ways, the only possible means for telling Effie and Essie from Ezra was by the tied-back horse-tail appearance of their flying long hair.

Mrs. Houghtaling had come recently from Fort Snelling with the lieutenant and their seven-year-old boy Jimmie, whose energies added many more units of power to that of the potent Norris children. She was expecting another child and slipped in and out of her quarters these days like a shawled shadow.

Mrs. Lane, the room-mate of the *Luella,* reunited with Lieutenant Lane, made the fourth of the other officers' wives. When in St. Louis she had cried to be with her husband. Now that she was here with him she shed tears daily for the parents in St. Louis.

"We have to be good friends, whether we want to or not," the colonel's wife chuckled. "There isn't another woman for miles around."

Strangely enough there were not many Indians here just now, only a few Crows and Peigans who seemed friendly and came in to trade. The colonel's wife said most of them were away hunting meat and berries. After the swarms of Indians at Fort Berthold it was a great relief, and, with more companies, the other women, and some formality in daily army life here, it made the whole place seem less wild.

Lieutenant and Mrs. Lane and Norman and Linnie took the children of the post fishing on one of those summer afternoons. They found the Judith a clear mountain stream, very beautiful, and what was more to the point, a great fishing spot. With grasshoppers for bait the women and children began landing fish as fast as the two men could hurry from one to another and take them off the hooks. But after several hours, during which Jimmie Houghtaling was fished out of the stream with consistent regularity, Ezra Norris was pried loose from a fish-hook, Effie was stung by a bee, and Essie had sprained her ankle in a hole, the adults went home in a fairly wrecked condition, although bearing much finny tribute to the officers' families.

But life during these days was not entirely made of such episodes.

All men who were not on guard duty were working at domestic tasks. Water had to be hauled from the river every day. Luckily the Missouri was clear here, and there was plenty of ice which had been put up the previous winter. There was no use digging a well, the colonel said: there was so much alkali in the soil that a spadeful turned and exposed to the sun soon looked as though it had soda sprinkled on it. One could hang a quarter of venison on a nail in the sunshine where it would dry but not spoil. Some of the men cut the wild hay and some brought wood, not only for present cooking needs but for the long cold winter ahead.

Once a hard rain came and most of the roofs leaked. Linnie found water coming through on to her dressing-table and bed so that she had to run with pans and pails to catch it. Mrs. Talcott told, with much shaking of her fat little body, how the colonel's dignity was upset when, taking a nap in his chair, the first few leaking drops in their quarters splashed into his open mouth and he thought he was drowning.

When the rain was over they could see that the peaks of the Bears Paw Mountains were covered with snow. It was summer's reminder that her stay —and Linnie's—were about up, here in the north.

There were only two boats left up the river, now, to come back down, the *Maybelle* and the *Luella*.

"I'll take whichever one comes first," she said.

"You ought to climb that high bluff separating the Judith from the Missouri before you leave and get the view from there," Norman suggested.

The two set out on that August afternoon. When they reached the highest point they found it to be a ridge about as wide as a wagon-track but so steep that they could throw a stone into the Missouri and then, facing about, throw one into the Judith. In truth, they amused themselves for a time with their throwing ability, using chips from the petrified wood they found there. Then they sat down on one of the logs, silently surveying the country before them.

It was Norman who broke the silence. "Nice up here, isn't it . . . the sky, the bluffs, the way the river runs below."

It came back to Linnie at once, that familiar phrase in the letter to Cynthia. "My love for you is like that." No matter what had happened between them in these friendly weeks, she was not to forget Cynthia.

She made no answer, merely asked at once if she might have his field-glass to see over the landscape.

But she had trouble with the focusing, could not make out anything.

"It's just all blurred, Norman."

"Let me show you." He took the glass, looking through it at the horizon as he adjusted it.

"Oh, let's go," he said impatiently. "Turning chilly."

How brusque he could be! And he had that snapping-to-action attitude she was beginning to know so well.

So, although she had not yet noticed the cold, without protest she went down the bluff with him, disappointed over the abrupt ending to the pleasant experience of an afternoon scarcely begun.

She put her hand in his while he helped her down several of the steeper places. Springing from the last of the stones before reaching the more level ground she felt a sudden bursting of something at her waistline and knew with all the horror of the ladylike times that a garment had cast connections and was on its way groundward.

"Oh, wait a minute ... I ..."

"What's the matter?"

"Something I wear ... it's ... I'm afraid it's coming off."

"Well, let it come." How cross he was.

"I can't. It's one of my ... my petticoats."

"Step out of it then."

"Oh, I couldn't do that . . . not here."

"To hell with your prissiness," he exploded. "Yank it off and be quick about it. The hills are full of Indians."

Chapter XIII

IT was like a journey in a nightmare, when one scarcely can move, that getting back into the shelter of the stockade.

Inside, after the interminable trip, they found the Indians had been sighted and the alarm given. There was intense excitement, with the women and children running to get together and every man hurrying to his post. The swivel guns in the bastion were manned. The officers came together in the sallyport with the women and children, all waiting that dreaded moment when the warriors would arrive.

Linnie, frozen with the horror of this bad dream from which there was no awakening, stood close to Mrs. Houghtaling, who had drawn her shawl tightly around her with the age-old instinct to protect her unborn child. The faces of the women held the same expression. It was as though all wore masks cast in one pattern, and the mold used for the casting had been fear.

Time, which usually moved so quickly, was standing still, waiting for this ghastly thing to happen.

As they stood there, tense of body, too frightened to speak, scarcely to think, the word went around that the Indians were not in war paint and there were a few women with them, clear indication that it was a marauding party and not a warring one. They had come within a quarter of a mile of the fort but suddenly had scattered and wheeled.

A detachment, sent out, found that a young soldier, herding, was dead with arrows in his body, and some of the beef cattle and a few horses had been stolen.

And now it was "Boots and Saddles!" A scouting detachment under Lieutenant Lane was despatched after them.

Mrs. Lane was hysterical with fear for her husband's safety, so Linnie went to her quarters and stayed a while, trying to quiet her with words that sounded more courageous than she really felt.

While she was there, the colonel's wife stopped long enough to say, "You better calm yourself, Mrs. Lane. If you had Mrs. Houghtaling's troubles you might have something to cry about."

The scare had brought Mrs. Houghtaling to childbirth prematurely, and only her husband and the colonel's wife were with her, for the doctor had gone with the scouting company. Mrs. Norris had taken Jimmie and packed him in her own close quarters with her three.

It was late when the men came back, empty handed, to report they had lost the marauders in the rough hills.

Norman was disgusted. "To think they can do that right under our noses... playing cat and mouse with the army. I'd like to help clean them all out."

In the morning Linnie found that the doctor had been with Mrs. Houghtaling the rest of the night after his arrival. The baby had lived only a few fleeting moments, as if a world of Indian fighting were too hard a life to face: killed by the Indians as surely as though an arrow had pierced its tiny body, she thought.

She went over to see Mrs. Houghtaling. And now she was confronted by a new kind of sorrow. That of the pilot's wife had been a silent dry grief. This was a frustrated one, the animal cry of the mother whose child was no more, a sobbing, indignant grief which blamed the place and the times and the hardships for her loss. Rachel in a frontier fort was crying for her children and would not be comforted.

Norman and Linnie went together to the brief services for the baby and the dead soldier held in a level spot of ground not far from the fort. The dry clumps of sage rattled as they walked. The August sun burned down on the hard packed ground. The dirt from the long grave and the short one already glistened white with its alkaline particles. Grasshoppers thumped on the big box and the little one.

Men stood bareheaded and bowed. The colonel read the burial service in his curt voice. The officers and soldiers and their wives joined in the prayer about the Lord's will being done. The sad sweet sound of *Taps* spilled its tears and its echo cried in the hills.

Linnie thought her throat would burst with its throbbing for the old mother whose soldier boy would not come home again, and for the young mother who could not think her dead baby was the Lord's will at all, but only the result of the evil of raiding Indians.

She had made two little wreaths of brown-centered daisies from the flowers on one of her summer hats. She put them now on the two mounds, one so large and one so tiny, but both so forlorn out here beyond the stockade.

Norman walked silently back toward the quarters with her. "I guess you won't want to prolong your stay after all this?"

"No...oh, no. I'm going on the very next boat. I think it's *terrible* to live like this...away from everything that's clean and pleasant and gracious and civilized."

The experience of the past two days had shaken her to the depths. She wanted to fly at life and pommel it with tight little fists. To change it and rearrange it so that human beings need not suffer so. She wanted to hurt Norman for his part in her hard lessons of life, for staying here in this barbarous country, for being the means of bringing her into contact with such heart-rending things. All the emotion of all the days behind her swelled now to one great cry: "Oh, why does life have to be this way?"

Her vehemence must have surprised him immeasurably. He looked at her quizzically for a moment and said no more.

The *Maybelle* and the *Luella* would be down soon. Mrs. Lane was in a constant state of indecision whether or not she, too, would take one of them. When she thought of leaving her husband she shed tears, but when she thought of her family in St. Louis she shed more.

And then the *Maybelle,* having shortened her trip, came in unexpectedly, and neither Linnie nor Mrs. Lane was ready. But the two, with practically every one who could walk, went down to the shore to look it over.

Norman talked with the captain and then came back where the young women were standing together.

"The captain will wait for you to get ready, Linnie. But I advise you to wait for the *Luella.* It's cleaner, larger, and—I'd say a better captain and crew."

So she and Mrs. Lane went on to the boat a few moments to see for themselves how it was and, finding it dirty, decided to wait.

The *Maybelle* had brought fresh vegetables from the Gallatin Valley, freighted from Helena to the river over the long journey. Norman bought potatoes at six dollars a bushel, and cabbage, turnips, and onions for thirty cents a pound. The next morning he concocted a box for river sand in which he packed some of these so they would keep for months.

"You shouldn't put down so much when your star boarder won't be here," Linnie advised.

"Just an old squirrel getting ready for a hard winter," he retorted.

A week went by with the new wine of the fall air a heady thing, blowing down from snow-tipped mountains. And the *Luella* did not come.

On an afternoon the Indians swooped down on the fort again, a larger band this time, more daring than before, their former successful conquests making them bolder. They brought that same terrifying fear to the women, that tenseness of body awaiting the outcome, and a weakness afterward as though one's strength had oozed from the very skin's pores.

This time they drove off more of the beef cattle and left another herder dead.

And now there was to be a larger expedition into the hills, with Norman heading it.

"Bolt the outside door," he told Linnie grimly. "And if there is any alarm go to the sallyport with the rest of the women."

It was a silent group which watched the men mount and ride forth. One never knew whether all would come back, or only part—or none.

Darkness came on.

Linnie lay long awake in that room which might have been Cynthia's. She knew by the lights and shadows of the night, by the quieting of the dogs' howling, by the dull agony of waiting, that it was very late.

She was following Norman every step of the way. His hard riding was her hard riding, his keen eye her own sharp one, his courage was her courage, his fatigue her own tiredness. It was as though she were not here at all, but only there beside him.

Then she heard dogs and horses and clanking metal and sprang up in bed, thanking a good God that the men were safe, praying that there would be no riderless horses. She had forgotten that the outer door was bolted, too, until she heard him calling her.

"Linnie . . . I'm here."

"I'm coming," she called back.

She threw on her quilted wrapper and got into her moccasins, lighted a candle and tried to wind her braids hurriedly around her head, but they would not stay. So when she unbolted the outer door and peered out above the flickering candle, shielding it with her hand, she felt shy to be in her wrapper with her loose hanging braids.

Norman did not come in. He only stood looking at her with no word. And then he said: "Put down your candle and come out and see the first northern lights."

It was breath-taking. There in the sky above the musty old timbers of the stockade rose a great delicate arch of golden filigree like the altar of a cathedral, on which soft candles of mauve and blue and pink threw up their pale light.

Together they stood and looked at those night fires in the sky. Norman put his arm around her and drew her close to his side, so that she could feel the hard steel muscles of his body. Both knew the moment had come.

"You're not going." He made it quietly—a definite statement without a note of questioning in it.

"No," she said simply, "I'm not going."

He kissed her then and this time the kiss was for herself and no other.

But before they went in Norman said: "There is one thing I should tell you—if we are to begin our married life with a clean slate."

"And that?" she asked happily, thinking of Cynthia, but not caring now.

"That last boat. The captain told me the *Luella* was tying up at Fort Benton for the winter. I knew all the time the *Maybelle* was your last chance to go."

She threw back her head and laughed at that.

"Every slate has two sides, you know. So if you're going to be particular . . . why . . . he told me that, too, Lieutenant."

Chapter XIV

AND now there was no barrier between them. Now she lay by his side the long cold nights. With silent but tacit understanding, nothing ever was said by either one about that daring adventure whereby she had come, unasked, up the river alone. It was as though she could not bear to speak of the bold thing she had done, now that the strange marriage was consummated. It was as though he sensed that in teasing her about the audacity of the journey he would lose her forever.

Squaw winter came on, that early cold spell of the autumn, with the first of the wild geese flying down the river like so many long-prowed boats suddenly taking to the sky. And then Indian summer followed with splashes of color on the hills and a bridal veil of haze over the valley.

Beginning at the guard-house which was Post Number One, the guard called the number of the post, the hour, and the old "All is well," Number Two taking it up until an answer had come from each guard.

On one of these crisp October nights, Number Four failed to respond, so that the relief was called instantly, and they found the soldier dead with an arrow in his body. A company under Lieutenant Houghtaling scouted far into the hills but could find no trace of the guilty. It angered every one that death could lurk about the post so constantly and go unpunished.

"Imagine the United States Army on the defensive." Norman was feeling it keenly. "Something's wrong about the method of handling the problem. Chase them into the hills a way ... they've scattered in every direction. Wear out your men and horses, and what've you accomplished?"

Since there had been so many hit-and-run attacks, the women no longer went outside the stockade. Every afternoon when they had "cleaned up" for the day, they put on their bonnets and shawls and strolled up and down the long common porch in front of their quarters as though they were on some pleasant boulevard, expecting to meet old friends at any moment. After this stroll one usually served tea to the other four, and the husbands dropped in sometimes to hash over the outside news which came in by wagon so long after it had happened.

Only now did Linnie receive the first letters from her relatives. Uncle Henry's gave her a hearty laugh. It was so much like him, puffed and pompous and full of the world's problems all duly settled in sweeping statements. But if his letter made her laugh, Aunt Louise's brought forth a tear or two and Cynthia's a deep blush. *Whatever happened? Where did you meet him? I should think it would*

*give you a very queer feeling, Linnie, after all you
knew about us....*

Yes, Cynthia was right. It did give her a very
queer feeling.

She looked around the four-room quarters where
there had been so many days of companionable living. Everything seemed as it should have been, as
though she and Norman were meant to be together,
laughing at the same things, mutually amused over
the post's small jealousies and sympathetic about its
troubles. But she did wish there never had been a
Cynthia in his life.

Norman had his constant duties: command of a
mounted detachment, preparation for inspections,
an occasional dress parade, sometimes acting as
officer of the day, attending officers' school certain
evenings. There were horses to be caught and
broken, with a hand burned severely on a rope for
part of his pains. But there were a few off-duty interests, too. Going hunting with other officers, he
killed a deer, killed a wild-cat another time, later an
elk.

As for Linnie, she worked energetically and happily in her miniature house, with the company laundress doing the washing and a soldier's wife coming
in for cleaning services. "Just to keep up the snob-
bish idea that officers' wives should employ servants," she laughed.

She had never been so happy. In spite of the hard
living, the inconveniences, the monotony of the com-

missary supplies, the rain coming in through a porous roof, she was happy. Because Norman seemed content.

Sometimes in the evening he would stretch out on the sitting-room cot, his long legs all but dangling over the ends, while Linnie, her dark coiled braids close to the kerosene lamp, read aloud to him— *Vanity Fair,* or the precious eastern magazines which brought a breath of a world so far away that almost they had forgotten it.

And sometimes she wondered, as all wives have wondered, whether he ever gave thought to his first love. Many times she decided to put away Cynthia's picture, eternally smiling at them from the white carved frame, but each time she forbore. No, she could compete with Cynthia. She, who was warm flesh and easy laughter, who could make appetizing stews, give sturdy advice for indecision and sympathy for disappointments, she had nothing to fear from the shadowy substance of a memory. Or so she thought.

And now a new interest came to her mind and she grew enthusiastic about the planning, that she would teach school there in the little sitting-room. It was as though life had given her so much in giving her Norman that she wanted to do something more for those around her than once she might have done.

"Why don't I, Norman? Effie and Essie and Ezra Norris and Jimmie Houghtaling . . . poor youngsters, running around here so wild, without regular lessons?"

Norman grinned. "*They* don't think they're 'poor youngsters.' I've a sneaking notion they prefer the running around."

And, indeed, four happier children in the whole country probably could not have been found. With the run of the garrison, several hundred soldiers for friends, an Indian pony, and no school, they lived in a childish paradise of freedom from restraint.

But Linnie talked to the parents, and nothing could have pleased them more than the planned regular hours. Mrs. Norris, contributing as she would three-fourths of the enrolment, was especially pleased.

"Three whole hours every day to know they're settled somewhere and not on top of the stockade or under a horse's hoofs."

Among the officers' families they dug up some McGuffy readers and a Ray's arithmetic, Hostetter's Almanac, Chase's Receipt Book, a Methodist hymnal, and an outmoded geography naming everything in the Colorado, Dakota, and Idaho territories as Nebraska Territory.

So Linnie started a little afternoon school in her quarters without benefit of diploma, teacher's certificate, school-board election, or salary. Norman made a crude blackboard for her, the chalk came in time on the long wagon trip from Fort Benton, and

Uncle Sam donated erasers cut from an old army blanket.

Effie, Essie, and Ezra and the seven-year-old Jimmie arrived every week-day at one o'clock, or at least with as much regularity as one could expect in the midst of such diversions as drills, sick mules, companies leaving on scouting trips, Indians arriving to trade, the drummer beating an occasional alarm, and cussing contests between two soldiers.

They even had a night program later in the unused officers' mess-hall where was stored some of the overflow from the commissary. In front of army blankets across an improvised stage the thoroughly drilled entertainers gave monologues, dialogues, and triologues, with scared Ezra Norris shouting: "I am stifling ... stifle, then ... when a nation's life's at hazard, we've no time to think of men." Only, in his embarrassment, forgetting Linnie's constant correction, he called it "stiffle" and "stiffling."

And then wild winds came down from the mountains, and snow clouds followed like so many rare white buffalo in panting herds, and the air was a smother of pulverized ice. The Indians were in winter quarters, and Norman said an Indian in winter quarters was not a warrior on the rampage but just a cold fellow who wanted to snuggle up to a fire and eat his squaw's cooking.

But that very night, as though some sensitive brave had overheard and wanted to refute the charge, the garrison was awakened by the drum beating a sudden and ominous alarm. The sawmill was burning, and all the men's work could not save it, so that by morning there lay only smoldering ruins. While Indians were suspected there was no proof. But after that, whenever they congregated at the post in their pretended friendliness, the commanding officer gave orders to allow a few of them to come inside. Norman said the colonel wanted them to see that they had enough men and arms to make it uncomfortable for any force they might bring.

Some of this show was a pretense, however. There was a lack of modern guns and not any too much ammunition if a great emergency should arise. New guns had been promised, but probably they had been sent to Laramie or some other place where the need seemed more urgent. Either that, Norman opined, or some one had slipped up on the shipping order, or red tape in Washington held them back.

The last of December—Christmas week—the winds and the blowing snows calmed, and only a biting below-zero cold settled over the valley.

On Christmas they had an improvised chimney for the children in the old mess hall, with Lieutenant Lane a too-slim Santa Claus but chosen as the only one who could get out of the opening in the shaky adobe structure. In fur cap and a coat made from an army blanket, both trimmed with red calico bands, and a deceased horse's tail for whiskers, he passed out gifts to all and sundry.

The biggest surprise of all came to Linnie from

Norman—a sewing-machine which had traveled by train, boat, and mule team to get there.

If she thought of the previous Christmas, the gift to Cynthia of her paid passage up the river and Norman's undying love with it, she put it aside as one tries to ignore an unwanted thing, giving her attention only to the wonder of her new machine and its intricacies, quite the envy of the other women.

Now she could make over her last year's dresses, turn and recut them like the *Godey* ladies whose silhouettes were pinned over the stove.

She must never lose contact with the outside world, she told herself. Although there was no place to go, she must keep as neat and fashionable as she could. So in the week following she tried her hair a new way, retrimmed her blue velvet hat of last winter, placing the bows smartly at the back instead of the front. Then she cut out some calling cards from heavy paper, printing her full name on them, and in her first made-over outfit called on Mrs. Talcott and Mrs. Norris, Mrs. Lane and Mrs. Houghtaling, with exaggerated company manners, leaving the cards, so that they all had a good laugh over her foolishness.

And now the year which had brought such an un-believable change in her life slipped away into its own Valhalla, and suddenly it was New Year's Day and 1868.

There were to be no lessons, and the five ladies

were to receive the officers in the colonel's quarters in the afternoon. It was quite exciting to put so much work and energy into preparations, with every one taking something from her own furnishings to make the quarters especially attractive.

"My two finest things are the big mirror and the new sewing-machine," Linnie laughed. "I can't carry the mirror, but we *could* have the new machine right in the middle of Mrs. Talcott's sitting-room."

All morning they labored in preparation, baking various kinds of cookies, making a weird punch over which they spent anxious moments of tasting, laying out their best clothes.

The men fell in with the elaborate plans and appeared in full uniform, so that all the women said they just wished Washington and New York society ladies could have seen those handsome officers and their not-so-bad-looking wives.

Then near tragedy struck. No one knew what caused it, but Ezra Norris, with his freckles, his shock of sandy hair, and his tough little body, was suddenly in a raging fever. Lung fever, the doctor said. He was afraid the boy couldn't get through.

It cast a gloom over the garrison. "Wish I hadn't teased him so much," Lieutenant Lane said. Hard-boiled Sergeant Smith ran the back of his hand across his nose. "I've cussed that ornery little skunk for getting under foot more times than one, but I never will again, so help me, if he'll get well."

Linnie thought she could not go on with the lessons, promised herself she would never scold about his mischievous ways again.

"Don't you think it would help more to have the girls here at their regular work?" Norman asked her. "Besides, no matter what happens, a soldier goes ahead with his duty. You're in the army now."

Yes, she was in the army, so she went ahead with her duty, seeing all the time that shock of sandy hair and that freckled face at the fourth cracker-box against the wall.

There came a day when the doctor stayed by the boy all the time. "If we had onions," he said, "hot poultices of them on his chest might help."

Only Norman and Linnie had onions left for flavoring the tough beef stews. Norman took them over to the hospital without delay, and no one knew whether they really were effective or whether the boy would have rallied anyway, but the turning point came in the night.

Every one told every one else. The garrison, like a single family, had a weight lifted from it. Linnie sang over her old smoky stove.

With the snows weighting down those flimsy roofs and the drill grounds a vast white tent without entrance, the soldiers took a notion to entertain by means of theatricals. Some of them had seen a good deal of fine acting, two had even done a little work on the boards, so their *Taming of the Shrew* was hilarious, with all the parts taken by men.

Katherine's voice emerged from the silk shawl swathed around her head as though coming up from the cradle of the deep, and the occasional switching of that shawl displayed two of the United States Army's hairiest legs. *Petruchio* rode in on a temperamental army mule. And when "one of the lords," returning from the hunt, stumbled over the prostrate form of the worst old soak in the garrison and exclaimed theatrically in Shakespearean words: "What's here? one dead or drunk?" the audience obligingly with one voice yelled, "Drunk!"

The last of the month the weather turned more bearable, and there was a sliding party with pancakes and hot coffee in Norman and Linnie's quarters afterward.

Ezra Norris, still a little pale under the brown-button freckles, came back to school. Lieutenant Lane began to tease him. Linnie scolded him heartily for his mischievousness. The sergeant cussed him out practically every day for getting under foot.

Norman was very busy on the board of survey now, in addition to his other duties. But they had many of their evenings alone, when Linnie read *Barnaby Rudge* aloud, or they made taffy or popped corn or sat and talked on a dozen different subjects pertaining to the world outside which was so very far away.

On Sunday evenings they always went to the old mess-hall to a service which any ordained minister would have said was sadly lacking in the essentials, for there was neither sermon nor prayer. The colonel went through a chapter from the Bible as though on a brigade charge, snapping off the melodious poetical psalms in the manner of field commands. Then they just sat and sang hymns. Linnie never had thought of herself as much of a singer, but now she was looked up to as the prima donna among them, her clear fresh voice soaring upward on the notes of "A mighty fortress is our God, a bulwark never failing."

And somehow this little group of people so far away from protecting civilization must have taken heart at the comforting words, must have felt a reassurance in the thought of that mighty fortress secure from all alarms. It was as though Washington might forget the guns and overlook the ammunition, but they still had God.

Chapter XV

FEBRUARY came in fairly mild. The snow tent on the drill yard, long since a dirty white, shrank until it lay flat on the ground.

In the last week a huge flock of birds with hoarse cries flew across the hills, so that Linnie said they made her restless, wishing she and Norman might follow them there, wherever they were going.

The thought of the spring to come brought a discontent with the cramped quarters, the dinginess of them, the rough whitewashed walls grown gray in the winter, the stove that smoked so irritatingly. She had an intense longing for a home, wide bedrooms, lovely gilt wallpaper, a stairway with mahogany handrail.

She talked to Norman about it, feeling very close to him now, so that she could even scold a little about household things which exasperated her.

"Are you going to stay in the service forever? Surely, Norman, you are so capable, you could do something where you wouldn't have to be under constant orders to go here, there and everywhere."

"Caught with the goods on. I own up that in the back of my mind I've sometimes had a plan. I believe the first time I can get leave of absence I'll go to Washington and see about the possibility of a later appointment there in the pension..."

He got no further, for Linnie was all enthusiasm. "Oh, Norman... to live in Washington. I'd admire..."

It was her turn now to get no further, for suddenly the words had a familiar sound.

I'd admire to live in Washington, Cynthia had said. And the excitement went out of her like a collapsed soap bubble, as it always did when she remembered Norman's deep love for Cynthia. She was never to forget that she must live forever on crumbs from the table.

Sometimes she tried to test his love in little ways as all women have done. After reading her diary, she would say: "This is the day of the month we went to the hills... you know... the time the Indians were coming."

"And you thought your petticoat more important than the Injuns."

"Just six months ago to-night we were... were really married, Norman. The night of the first northern lights."

But he would never be romantic, only saying dryly: "Uh-huh. Haven't noticed any since."

No, Norman did not love her as he had loved Cynthia. She had tried to make herself believe he did, but it was not true. She must face it, must always remember that it was Cynthia who held his heart. But when they were cozily settled on these

still-cold evenings with the two lamps lighted and
a log fire, or when she lay safely by his side hearing
the harsh sounds of the coyotes in the distant hills,
she forgot her doubts and fears and thought only
that she was meant to be his wife.

And then March suddenly was here, with very
little evidence of spring, for the snows came on
again and the children all waded down the long
common porch to Linnie's quarters for lessons, Essie
and Effie as boyish in copper-toed boots as Ezra and
Jimmie.

Raids by the Indians were sporadic, but there was
a constant succession of thieving—cattle, corn, a
horse or two—more a subject for irritation than
alarm. Norman said the new guns would come
through as soon as spring came. When the marauders got a taste of those they wouldn't try it a second
time.

Almost before they could realize it, the spring
thaw started in good earnest, and miniature Missouri and Judith rivers sloshed all over the drill
grounds.

The last week of the month every one who could
do so went down to see the ice go out. They found
the river in torment, twisting and turning in the
agony of her torture, moaning with sick voice, then
breaking suddenly into a sharp cry when the splintering of the ice wracked her.

"But though the ice separates us . . . the river runs
below. My love for you is like that," Linnie repeated

it to herself as though it were a remembered quotation from some famous writer instead of the troth Norman had plighted to Cynthia.

There she was again going back to Cynthia. She wondered why she was doing that foolish thing so much lately, when she had been almost free from thoughts of her in the winter.

For fifteen hours the river endured its travail, and then the ice went out and only the river ran below.

Norman was wanting to go to the coal bank on the other side, and now he could cross over in a few days, the still ice-cold water so free from large cakes that any danger had passed.

He started at six one morning in the yawl. In the late afternoon, while he was gone, supplies and mail came in by wagon from Fort Benton, and there was much excitement. It was always a big event, and Linnie was sorry Norman was away, with all the outside news from the drivers and with the magazines, papers, and letters to sort and read.

They said the Senate and President Johnson were fighting over Secretary Stanton, who was sitting tight in his office day and night with a military guard, and there was talk of impeaching the President. Goodness! Up here in this little world you almost forgot there was a President and a Senate.

And now suddenly she knew the reason for that continual recurrence of thought about Cynthia. It was a premonition. For there was a letter from Uncle Henry. And George Hemming was dead. He had been killed in a railroad wreck on his way to Chicago, where he was going to buy goods. They thought the rails had buckled under the constant cold. Cynthia was taking on dreadfully, and he was quite put to it to know what to do for her. Aunt Louise couldn't lift her head off the pillow. Olga had to wait on them both. He wished she were there to be with them.

Linnie experienced shock at the news and felt a warm deep sympathy for them all. They were her people and they were in trouble.

George was dead. No more cutting-up. No more jokes on people. No hi-jinks ever again. She could not imagine him lying still and unsmiling.

And then almost immediately she was remembering something else. How would Norman take this news? Cynthia was free now and—

But she would not let herself peer further into the darkness of the thought, turning quickly away from that part of her mind as one turns away from the door of a room in which some frightful object lies.

She dreaded the telling—feared so much the reading in his face of something she did not want to see —that when he came, wet and hungry from the long trip, she did not give him the news at once, saving it for later in the evening.

He had bought a young cow and was full of talk about having plenty of milk and butter later. When he was in fresh clothes and had eaten the good beef stew, dumplings, and dried apple pie, asking her how she could make such a good one out of those pieces of rubber, and was smoking, with his feet on the hassock, she did not want to break the charm of his comfort. And because she had not done so at once and the telling had grown harder—so important a thing without possibility of excuse for forgetting— she did not tell him at all.

April arrived on an east wind, cool and dry with scudding clouds in the blue and spring smells up from the river. And Linnie had not told. She hated herself for her cowardliness, tried to make herself promise that now she would tell him. But as there had been neither boat nor wagon train with mail, he would see that she had known it for days. And with the knowledge must come the reason why she had kept silent, and that he should never know. He was her husband. Nothing could come between them. If she believed that, why did she not tell him at once, she questioned, and had to admit it was because she was afraid to know the truth.

The children were restless this afternoon. Part of it she realized might be due to her own vague disturbance. And it was April Fool. Essie and Effie had worn Ezra's clothes with the wild notion that it was an April Fool joke, but so tomboyish were they in their usual characters that the mere donning of trousers made very little difference in results, although Linnie sent them home to change at once because of the shamefulness of it.

When they returned, clothed, if not in their right minds, their arithmetic lessons were atrocious.

Jimmie Houghtaling made of his reading lesson a race to reach the last period without regard for any others en route.

In answer to the question about naming the chief river in India, Ezra said, "Hades," which brought roars from his sisters.

Linnie said to herself that the poor youngster had heard more about Hades from tough old soldiers than he ever had about the Ganges.

Just after the four had left, with Linnie more relieved than usual at their going, Norman came in. He had news, having been ordered to hold himself in readiness to go in command of a party to find a wagon-road to the mouth of the Musselshell River. It was all in preparation for a company to spend the summer there in tents with grazing stock.

"Maybe it's an April Fool joke," Linnie suggested, always worried about orders, always fearful that those perilous trips might find no home-coming because of storm or wild animal or arrow.

"The army doesn't joke," Norman shrugged a shoulder. " 'Orders is orders.' "

After a full day of preparations he was ready to start with twenty-five men, including the doctor and an interpreter.

"How long will it be, Norman?"

"I doubt if much more than a week, but don't sit

and watch the clock. You know how things are in this country by now...all kinds of delays."

"Come back safe." She clung to him, apprehensive now only for his physical safety.

Bring him safely back, no matter what follows after that. Let him come back unharmed and I'll tell him about Cynthia the minute he gets here. Thus did she try to bribe God into watching over the one she loved.

All the days that followed were dreary ones and anxious. There was never a chance to hear in any way from these excursions into the dangerous hills. There was nothing to do but shut the eyes of one's imagination to flying arrows from ambush, the ears to the sounds of hard-riding ponies, the nostrils to that queer Indian-and-buffalo-hide odor which to her dying day brought distaste to her senses.

The days passed with the children coming in for lessons. She sewed, did the housework, tried to read. But always her ear was listening for the thud of hoofs and the clank of metal.

The week went by and they had not come. On the eighth day it started raining. The rain turned to sleet, the sleet to snow. All night the winds howled and raged, and the snow blew. In the morning a six-inch blanket lay over the post like a shroud over dead soldiers.

Linnie thought she could not stand the anxiety longer. So she got into Norman's older buffalo fur coat and, with high lifted skirts, made her way to the colonel's quarters.

Dumpy Mrs. Talcott, her fat face as placid as a summer moon, told her to stop her worrying, everything was probably all right.

"My, my," she clucked, "if you're going to live to be an army wife as old as me, you'll have to take things calmer than this. Now go back and cook a big kettle of stew and sing at the top of your voice. There's nothing like the smell of something cooking and the sound of your own voice to keep up your spirits."

So Linnie went back to her work and her singing:

> *Oh do you remember the Indian tale*
> *Of the maidens who wept by the creek in the vale*
> *For the braves who were slain in Nehawka?*

There, she was singing about Indians when she couldn't even bear the sight of them.

She put a piece of frozen beef rump on to cook and pared potatoes and withered turnips. Strange, how it did relieve her!

> *And the little creek fed by their weeping all day*
> *Rose into a river that wended its way*
> *To the sea with the tears from Nehawka.*

Suddenly she sensed for the first time the deeper import of the Indian legend.

Women everywhere wept for their men. Black or

white, red or yellow! It didn't seem possible that a woman of another race could think of her man as she thought of Norman. But probably it was true.

Tears were all alike then. How queer that was! There was no racial quality in them. All the tears that had been shed by women since the world began —what a deep stream they made!

Chinese women's tears—Negro women's tears— white women's tears—*rose into a river that wended its way to the sea with the tears from Nehawka.*

The snow ceased and the sun came out. Nine days, ten, eleven, twelve, and the clouds gathered again like a hostile tribe renewing its attack. The snows came in great sheets of hard sleety crystals, turned into a whipping, blinding blizzard.

Renewed worry clutched her, and neither cooking nor singing could overcome it. She walked to the small windows time and again, scraped away the frost, and peered out into the white blankness.

The fear of her own heart gave her sympathy for all men everywhere, for those on the high seas and in the hill countries and in desert places; made her sensitive to the anxiety of all women whose menfolks were not safe under the home roof.

"Take care of every one, everywhere," she pleaded with the God of storms, "all the men who have to go away from home and the women who watch for the first dear sight of them."

Thus did she come to feel that all women's tears are alike. And thus did she come to know how army

wives sense universal sorrow and acquire understanding.

Then quite suddenly on an early evening she heard
pounding of hoofs, barking of dogs, clank of harness, and lusty shouts. Peering out she saw flickering
lanterns. Even then, one never knew. Often there
was a riderless horse or no horse and rider at all.

So she stood in the middle of the floor, unmoving,
her hands at her throat, tight-clenched, until there
was a sound at her own door and Norman came
stumbling in from the snows.

*Oh, thanks be to God for taking care of men who
go away and of women who watch for their coming.*

Chapter XVI

NORMAN was safe home again to the fire and to dry clothes and a hot supper.

When he had eaten enough for two men after the lean days and was comfortable with a pipe, he began telling her of the hazardous trip, quite volubly for one who was never very talkative.

It made Linnie think of him as a young boy who had saved all the relating of his adventures for his mother. It gave her, for the first time, a maternal feeling toward him.

That first Saturday they'd marched eighteen miles, he told her, and camped at Dog Creek, after a lot of trouble with the pack-animals. Went over the poorest country he'd ever seen the next day. Dry soil, as soft and loose as a plowed field, no vegetation but sage and cactus. Came to a dry creek, found some wood and a little strong alkali water in a hole in the creek bed.

Then came the day of the hard rain that turned to snow. So dark they couldn't see anything, but they kept moving, hoping to find a good camping-place. When the storm passed, found they had traveled twelve miles but made very little progress in the right direction. That was the night the sentinel fired at Indians. Rode down the creek bed about five miles, then over the worst of the Bad Lands. Went on until they found a little scant grass for grazing. Saw five grizzly bears and did twenty-two miles that day.

As he was sitting there, talking to her so freely and so fully about all that he remembered, she watched him, only half aware of the details he was giving her. *He's forgotten her entirely,* she was thinking. *He's all mine. I'm everything to him now. Nothing could come between us.*

He was filling his pipe again, talking on. Well, that's the way it went; traveling six, eight, ten miles maybe, with snow so dense some days you could hardly see where you were going. Slept on the ground every night with no cover but blankets. One day they struck the wagon-trail from Helena and got to the mouth of the Musselshell about the same time the rain and a big bunch of Crow Indians did. Guards never took their eyes off the Crows. Camped in the river bottom a mile from Fort Hawley.

Got up every morning at two-thirty or three. One day couldn't move at all on account of the snow-storm. Had to cut young cottonwood trees for the horses to eat. Built a shanty of cord-wood and covered it with the blankets. Met the agent of the Northwestern Fur Company who gave him an extra buffalo robe. Then the agent of the Overland Mail Company came in. He'd been attacked by the Sioux, one of his men lost, all the horses killed. Gave him a horse and told him he better stay with Uncle Sam.

He was stretching his long arms above his head, tired after the strenuous days, luxuriating in the good old warmth of the log fire.

I've made it happy and pleasant for him. It's all turned out right.

Linnie should see Fort Hawley. No, at second thought, she shouldn't. Never saw such a dirty place overrun with Indians and their dogs. Although he let some of the men go over, he and the doctor preferred sitting by their own camp-fire. Such a time as they had drying blankets after some of the snows! Then after that there was mud.

Followed the divide between the Missouri and Crooked Creek and met a party of eighteen Crows. Saw them first, so got the advantage of them, which made them very friendly. That's what the old U.S. Army was pretty good about ... see the other fellow first and forestall him.

Camped on Amel's Creek—plenty of wood and water there. Climbed a high bluff of pine and cedar to get a view of the country and see how to proceed in the morning. Saw lots of bear tracks. Got out of the Bad Lands and followed the main divide between the Missouri and Judith mountains. Cooked supper with sage weed after a twenty-five mile day. Then to-day got up with this snow falling and wind strong and tramped eighteen miles through the blizzard. And now at home.

"Gosh, Linnie," he caught her hand and pulled her down on the chair's arm. "After that trip this looks like ..." he glanced around at the homely old quarters made less homely by her deft hand "... Buckingham Palace."

She did not want to, oh, how she did not want to break the charm of the home-coming, but she had made a promise and must keep it.

"I hate to tell you something, Norman." She ran tender fingers over his hair. "It will bring back ... the past ... and all. But I had a letter from Uncle Henry. And ... Cynthia is in trouble ... George Hemming is dead."

And when he did not say anything, she told him everything of her own accord, how it happened, and all that Uncle Henry had written.

When she had finished, Norman put her aside and got up. He tapped his pipe carefully.

"I'll write my report of the trip now."

No, there never was any way to tell what Norman was thinking.

Life went on as it had done before those weeks of separation. Norman was very busy. There were charges against two privates and the two court-martials, writing the proceedings, special requisitions for clothing to be made, as well as all his regular duties.

Linnie cooked the best meals she could for him with her limited list of supplies. There was plenty of food in the commissary. Uncle Sam had no intention of letting his regulars starve, but the list of items which could be packed and sent to this out-of-the-way post was very short. So she was compelled to use the same things constantly. Canned tomatoes which had been overpurchased came to her table in every known guise. They were soup. They were stewed with dried bread crumbs, baked with dumplings, sweetened with dark molasses for dessert.

"I can see right through you," Norman would address the meal's main dish. "Don't you try to deny it. You're a tomato."

Butter was the worst trial. "It usually outranks the commanding officer," Norman said.

So now with the fresh young cow they tried making their own. The first was so thin they spooned it on to their bread, the second so salty it might have come out of the brine barrel. The third churning was so good they congratulated each other all through the meal.

Once when Norman seemed particularly cheerful over the treat of a custard pie (made without eggs) she thought it a good time to broach a subject close to her heart. "Norman, what if it turns out you are one who has to go to the Musselshell?"

"Well...what if it does? 'Orders is orders.'"

"Oh, Norman...not to be gone all summer!"

"Three months isn't so long."

"But if you do have to...what do you think about my going back east?"

"I don't think much about it, Missy. It would take all the summer to get down and back."

In spite of her disappointment, it brought comfort to her. She was glad he didn't want her to go.

Not once in these weeks had he mentioned Cynthia's widowhood. Sometimes when he was talkative about post events or news from the outside or grinned with her in a light-hearted moment, Linnie decided he had not given it much thought and chided herself for her fear that now in his heart he might wish he had waited for the girl he wanted. But sometimes when he lapsed into those long silences in the evening with his pipe, looking into the fire as though lost in memories, her heart beat cruelly with the pain that he was remembering his love for Cynthia as strong and as sure as the river which runs below.

If only he would say: "Poor Cynthia. I thought a lot of her once."

Let something happen to make me know he is contented, was her wish. *Give me some sign by which I could know he would choose me even if he had the chance of choice.* But the answer to her prayer never came.

The long-expected new guns finally arrived, but the ammunition for the artillery was not in the shipment. Some one had slipped up again, or red tape had held it back, but no excuses could smooth over the exasperation of the officers.

"We can throw hot tomato stew on the Injuns if they attack," Norman said in disgust.

And then Linnie's fears were realized. It was Norman who had orders to hold himself in readiness to take two companies to the Musselshell. The men packed to move. But even before they started, orders were held up for a day when a band of marauding Indians came in and drove off more horses and mules. It was getting to be such an old story, that chase into the hills with nothing but tired men and horses for reward.

For the movement to the Musselshell, Norman was placed in charge of the mounted detachment to go overland, twenty-five men, a guide and interpreter, mules and extra horses, as well as the beef cattle to be herded in grassier places. All others were to go in flatboats.

There was something of a tumult on the day of this egress. The men in the flatboats pulling away, the mounted detachment in readiness for their orders, the yelping of dogs, the rounding up of restless cattle, all made an unusual commotion.

Women and children were out to watch the departure. Lessons had been omitted, and Effie, Essie, Ezra, and Jimmie were in a perpetual state of being yanked back from some place in which they were not supposed to be.

Seeing Norman ready to go, it broke over Linnie afresh, in a great protesting wave, that she could not be here three months without him. All at once the long weeks of loneliness in the dingy quarters, the hours of anxiety, the fear of attack, the inconveniences, the monotony of the food, seemed more than she could bear.

She clung to his arm. "Norman, I want to go with you! I could hurry and get ready. I could live in a tent."

When he laughed at that, she said "I mean it. Please let me. The minute you go away I can't stand it here."

"I'm flattered, Mrs. Stafford! Why, that's a poem."

But she would not smile. "If anything happens to you . . ."

When he saw how upset she was, he drew her to him, smoothed her hair.

The tears came then, and no doubt he thought they were only for the summer's coming loneliness, not understanding a woman. But they were not for the loneliness to come so much as for the constant questioning of her heart.

He kissed her tenderly, lifting her chin in his gloved palm. "Now . . . now! Why, you're an army wife. You must be a good soldier."

She dried her eyes so he would not carry away the memory of her in tears.

"I'll try."

"You make me feel selfish. Maybe you should have gone down east."

"I'll be all right."

"I'll tell you what . . . I'll ask for leave of absence to take effect when I come back."

"That will be nice."

"It's only for three short months. Can you stand it?"

She tried to smile. "I can stand it."

The bugle rang clear in the summer morning.

There was a clank of metal and pounding of hoofs. Norman waved back to her. She waved to him as long as she could see him. Then she turned and ran to her quarters so that no one would talk to her.

Chapter XVII

So Norman was gone. And that night Linnie bolted both doors and lay shivering as though it were midwinter instead of a spring night with a new moon caught on the tip of a green hill and a bittern calling for its mate.

There seemed so little incentive to get up and eat and tidy the quarters. She made herself go through the motions and even schooled herself to put her whole mind on the children's lessons, for she had told the mothers there would be classes until the middle of June.

But the day was springlike and fairly shouted for them to come out, so they began a lengthy pleading with teacher to get up a fishing party at the Judith instead of the lessons, as they had done last summer. It ended with a trip to the colonel to see if they would be allowed to do it.

The colonel, who had more heart than his crusty exterior evidenced, and who may have remembered a long-gone day of his own with rod and bent pin thought it might be all right but said they must have a bodyguard.

There was a full hour then of excited preparations, getting out all the old cottonwood poles, the lines and tin cans for the bait.

"Why, they're *tomato* cans," some one said in surprised tones, to bring a laugh.

Then the little group of youngsters set forth from the sallyport escorted by an officer father, a mother, Linnie, and four soldiers.

"The fish will be scared to death when they see the whole United States Army coming," Linnie said gaily, so there was ready laughter from every one again.

And then, they saw them. Indians. It was almost simultaneous with the sound of the alarm by the guard. Still a mile or so away they were coming over the hills south of the fort.

Like the snapping of a bow cord, laughter was broken off, and the children pushed hurriedly back into the comparative safety of the stockade.

"Can't we go?" Jimmie Houghtaling kept repeating, his childish mind unable to cope with the sudden change.

As the Indians came nearer they were seen to be painted and mounted for war, no women or children with them. This was no mere marauding party. Orders were snapped. The swivel-guns in the bastion were manned, and every regulation for defending the fort was carried out, as the warriors circled around all sides except the river one.

The commanding officer took ten men and rode out to parley, but the answer to their friendly gesture was a volley of arrows. They returned immediately, and as soon as they were inside, the sallyport was closed. Lieutenant Houghtaling had an arrow in the fleshy part of his hip and was put at once on an improvised bed on the floor. Mrs. Houghtaling, distraught, expecting a child again, stood by him, her arms about Jimmie.

The other women and children huddled together in a group, fright frozen.

Linnie kept thinking, "This is it ... now it's here," and even wondered at her own calmness, not realizing that fear had deadened her emotions. She could hear the booming of the cannon on the bastion and suddenly remembered how the ammunition for them had not come.

The colonel came up and put his hand on his wife's arm. "You remember what I've always told you, Mother." He spoke as briskly as ever.

And stocky Mrs. Talcott, white-lipped, and with her ready laughter stilled now, said coolly as though it were an ordinary thing, "I remember, Colonel. Only," she caught his hand, "if it happens, I want you to be the one."

"I'll be the one."

Then he turned to Linnie. "If there is no way out but capture, Lieutenant Stafford wants you to be shot by one of our officers before surrender. Lieutenant Lane would do so," he snapped and left.

Surrender—death—shot—death. The words went around in circling rotation but with no meaning.

She tried to think consecutively, to say something to any one near, that she might hang on to sanity, but there was no lucid thinking in her. Just *surrender— shot—death.*

Then something seemed to bring back mental saneness. Ezra Norris, too old to be in any one's arms, too young to be anything but a frightened little boy in a world of tragic horror, stood there alone, apart from his sisters who were crying and clinging to their mother. His face was so pale that the freckles stood out on it like brown painted spots and his quivering lips were set in an endeavor to keep up a brave front.

It touched some chord in her which responded to that childish attempt at courage. He, too, had been told to be a good soldier.

She took his hand and pressed it. And his own, clammy with the perspiration of his fear, pressed back in silent understanding.

Strangely enough his loud scared rendition of the piece he spoke that night came back to her. *When a nation's life's at hazard, we've no time to think of men.* And the remembering gave her a fleeting measure of comfort and strength.

They could hear the war yells and the reverberation of the guns. After a time both ceased. Some one in the group whispered that the artillery ammunition had given out. The whisper passed down to Linnie. The silence was worse than ever the noise had been. All the women and children were kneeling there together. *A mighty fortress is our God.*

And then the word came. The Indians had taken to the hills just as the last firing of the swivel guns was possible. Several must have been killed but, tied on their ponies as they were, there was no way of knowing how many.

"*Now* can we go fishing?" Jimmie was asking. And the childish attitude after so painful a time relieved the tension as nothing else could have done.

The fright was over, so that every one could scold about the ammunition. But the colonel, tight-lipped, a good servant of his country, said nothing.

Chapter XVIII

THE great scare was over, but then came a new agony for Linnie. During the time of her fright she had thought only of the immediate danger here at the post, but now some one was recalling that the Indians had come from the direction in which the men had gone only twenty-four hours before and was questioning the fate of the mounted detachment.

She hurried over to her own quarters, bolted her doors, and sat down on the edge of the bed, staring with unseeing eyes at the whitewashed wall of the little room.

In imagination she followed those twenty-five men riding down the river valley. They had camped at Dog Creek just as Norman had laid out the trip. Then to-day they had been going over that poor country, that "dry soil as soft and loose as a plowed field, no vegetation but sage and cactus" of which he had told her. Open country. And this early afternoon they had been attacked. Hundreds of those painted devils against twenty-five. Norman lay dead somewhere on that "dry soil, soft and loose as a plowed field."

For a long time she did not stir from the bed's

edge or take her eyes from the dingy wall. Then, almost as plainly as though they were spoken words, she heard them: "Be a good soldier."

With supreme effort she pulled herself up from the depths of her agonizing. This wasn't being a good soldier. Other people besides herself were anxious. Other women were having more trouble than her own. Mrs. Houghtaling whose husband had an arrow in his hip, with the doctor on his way to the summer camp: what about her?

So she washed her hands and face as though the doing so might wash away her selfish worry. Then she went over to the hospital.

She found that the lieutenant's arrow had been cut out by that old Indian-fighting Sergeant Smith in lieu of the doctor and one could only hope luck had guided the hard old fellow's hand and the cleansing of the wound afterward. Then she got Jimmie and took him back to her own quarters to play checkers with him.

They were in the midst of the second game when word came that a boat was in.

It was the *Sallie*, the first to come up, and it brought word of the men. There was even a hasty note from Norman written the morning before saying they had passed Bird Rapids and were all well. Only thing that had gone wrong, three mules fell into the river, getting their packs all wet. Since they had passed the rapids, the colonel thought they had not encountered the warring Indians. So Norman

was not dead. He was alive and had written her the
first letter she ever received from him. It ended:
"Hope you are getting along all right. We will look
forward to a leave of absence when I get back. Ac-
cept my love and respect. Norman."

Love and respect! He loved her. And even though
unasked she had come up the river to him, he re-
spected her. She would not let herself compare the
note with those love letters of Cynthia's she had
heard read. But she put it in the front of her flowered print where it crackled happily against her
breast, and there she kept it for days.

Boats came up fairly often now. The *Arrowsmith*
brought her word from Norman that they were
settled in their tents after arriving in an uproar.
The trip below Bird Rapids had been a bad one.
Rained all day and all night, and the road had been
the worst he ever traveled. In two places they had
to dig a road with butcher knives. Cattle mired
twice. Lots of thunder and lightning. Left the bluffs
and the river above Fort Hawley and started across
for the Musselshell. A trader came out from Fort
Hawley to report Indians on the rampage and advised going to the fort to camp. Went ahead anyway.
Just got here to camp now on the sixth day and
found the men in flatboats had arrived first and had
been attacked. Indians had been driven off now.
Men were at work on stockades. Had just opened
the box she packed and found her pins, socks, buttons, and the needles already threaded. She was a

real army wife. She mustn't forget to be a good soldier.

But it was hard to be a good soldier all those lonely summer months. Only by keeping herself busy and looking forward to Norman's return was she able to rise above the constant fear for safety, the ugly distractions, the alkali dryness of the ground, the smells from the stables, the rancid butter, the small jealousies among the wives. Mrs. Houghtaling, nervous and irritable in her condition, was feuding with Mrs. Lane, chronically homesick and teary. Each one came to Linnie with her minute grievances concerning the other.

And now a new fear presented itself. Rats had come in by steamer, and this summer they had multiplied about the garrison until one met an ugly scudding creature at almost any time and place. They ate the stored grain and got into the commissary. They filled her with loathing dread, and sometimes in the night she awakened to sit up and listen to horrible scratching feet in the outside walls. Between slinking Indians and slinking rats, she thought at times she preferred the savages.

No more Indians had attacked, but that eternal vigilance was nerve-wracking. And the thought of danger to the men in their tents at the Musselshell never left her waking hours.

Talk of new treaties percolated into the garrison —with the Blackfoot, up at Fort Benton, with the Crows at Fort Hawley—but what was a treaty? So far, a thing to be broken excepting in a few instances.

To take up her time she planned how she could refurbish her clothes if Norman ever applied for that leave of absence. Now that boats were coming up occasionally, she lived for the mail. The arrival of her *Ladies' Repository* was more than an advent. It was an event.

That month Norman sent two more letters. She read them over until she knew them by heart. The Indians had attacked the herd a half-mile from camp and killed the two privates herding, Ivesnil and Cook. The body of Cook couldn't be found, but from marks and blood on the bank it was supposed that he jumped into the river. Fifteen men had searched for the body. The sutler had landed a lot of liquors and had to ship them out again by orders. Five steamers had passed up now, but only the *Cora* had gone down. Yes, he had sent it—an application for six months' leave.

Her eyes grew wide at the startling news, and they must look again to see that the reading had been correct. How like Norman to have saved that wonderful thing until the very last and then to have written it as though it were a tacked-on postscript.

Now there was something to do in earnest. She pulled her machine out into a good light and laid out every dress and hat she possessed in order to make the most of her wardrobe. She studied the *Godey* ladies as though her very life hung on panels and pleats, and the fact that she possessed no wide silk fringe, such as they were wearing, took on the weight of a catastrophe.

Norman's letters dwindled, for boats did not come up as frequently as in those first weeks. But when the letters came they were filled with his constant activities. He had arrested two men for selling liquor to Indians and had broken up another bunch at a woodchopper's ranch. News had come up from Forts Stevenson and Buford that the Indians were unusually bad. He and some other men had gone up into the bluffs to get a flagstaff for the Fourth of July. Worked hard to get it across the river and then lost it by a huge drift of wood coming down. Two soldiers had deserted by going downriver on the company's raft. Made a new raft and got another flagpole and raised the flagstaff at retreat, hoisting the stars and stripes at reveille on the morning of the Fourth. Made him wonder if anywhere in the Union there had been harder work to get the flag up.

And then in late July he wrote that four white men in a woodchopper's cabin not far away had been killed after the Indians had torn down the cabin. So he and a detachment had been skirmishing through timber and brush but had found only pipes, dried beef, paint, a large knife, and moccasins hidden under a bank.

It took all the enjoyment out of her dressmaking. Norman scouting through brush and timber for those painted things who knew brush and timber so much better than he!

And the very last day of the month a letter said the Crows with their changeable policy were pouring into camp near the army for protection against the Sioux who were after them. They were a nuisance, too, into every crack and crevice outside the stockade. Last night he had spent some time on the bastion with the guard as there were signal fires on the hills!

At that she gave up trying to sew, her nerves too much on edge. Oh, why wasn't Norman a lawyer or a doctor or a hand-organ grinder instead of in this awful army?

August had to be lived through before he would break camp, and when no boat and so no letter came, she thought she could not stand it to have had that last letter end on its note of danger. Those signal fires on the hills! Had they called for the Sioux to attack?

Sometimes she walked the floor in her nervous thinking. But when another letter came on a little stern-wheeler, he was still safe, although the latest development was that a detachment of the soldiers sent overland to Fort Peck had been attacked and pursued by a large band of Indians. The irony was that the Crows and the Sioux had kissed and made up and joined in hostilities against the whites. He could write her no more as they were breaking camp to-morrow. She was not to look for him very soon as the going up with the flatboats would be long and tedious.

All that long wait before they could get back, weeks maybe!

Then she found a new interest besides the dressmaking. Mrs. Houghtaling gave birth to a daughter. Lieutenant Houghtaling, who had suffered a long-drawn-out siege of fever after his arrow wound, was still in the hospital when the baby came. So Linnie went back and forth between the parents, carrying messages and sometimes the baby herself. The care of young Jimmie was divided among the various officers' families, with motherly Mrs. Talcott general overseer and only young Mrs. Lane complaining about the extra work it put upon her.

The almanac over the kitchen stove said September was here at last. The mail came in, and the leave of absence was standing on the clock shelf like the passport to Paradise.

Linnie thought she could not endure it until Norman would come and have the pleasure of its opening. Every day was a painful waiting because each one brought less chance of a downriver boat. And not to take the river trip meant that long roundabout drive over the rough road to Fort Benton which Norman said followed the headwaters of the streams flowing into the Missouri from the north, and then the long long ride to Helena, and thence by stage to the end of the Union Pacific.

But the September days came and went, and Norman did not come. She grew frightened at the long delay. The last boat—the *Benton*—went down. The weather grew foggy and cold. It rained. The wind blew constantly, then stilled, and there was a tissue-paper thickness of ice on the river. The leave of absence sat up on the clock shelf unopened.

Twenty-two days of September had gone by, and then there were unusual shouts and barking of dogs, bawling of cows, clanking of metal, and much activity in the stockade. The men had come.

And here after a time was Norman, brown as a Piegan Indian himself, his arms around her and a kiss for her so ardent that it brought overwhelming happiness to her.

She could scarcely get the unplanned meal, could not think what to do or to cook in the joyful confusion over his coming.

When he had been in and out a half-dozen times, seeing to necessary duties in connection with the return of the men and stock, he got into dry clothes and they ate the first meal together for nearly four months. Afterward, he wiped the dishes for her and she glowed with pleasure at the extra attention, so seldom did he do anything of the sort. While he made hard work of it and got clumsily in her way as he stepped around the little room, he told her of the long trip home.

So many things had happened which seemed unbearable, but he always managed to come out on top some way. Only one really bad thing. Old O'Malley, the blacksmith, had been drowned. No one knew just what happened. They had been putting the flatboats into the water preparatory to breaking camp, and the old fellow had disappeared. They found his body, but it was too late. Yes, they buried him there at the bluff, marked it as well as they could. Now a letter must be sent back to his family in the States.

"Poor O'Malley, always talking about going back some time to see his folks. Just a few nights before it happened, we were sitting around the fire and he got to talking about them. Said if he could 'just walk in the kitchen again and smell apple-pie and cinnamon,' he'd die happy."

Well, that was one thing. Then he, himself, ran a fish horn into his foot and a sort of inflammation set in.

But when Linnie was all anxiety over that, he made light of it, saying the worst trouble was sandbars! Wrestled with them all the time. Worst of all was when one of the boats started leaking very fast and they had nothing handy to caulk it with, so he yanked off his shirt, tore it up, and stuffed it in.

"Oh, Norman, that was a *good* shirt."

"It was a good boat," he retorted, and they had a moment of happy laughter together, which made Norman say: "Gosh, it's good to be back home."

Home! For a moment Linnie let her glance wander around the rooms. Why, how strange! They did look nice to-night. The good ingrain carpet, the robes over the army cot, the little stand with books, the two lamps casting a glow on the big mirror. Queer, they had not looked so good last night. But last night Norman was not here. To-night he was here. And now it was home.

"Well, let's see, what else would you be interested in? Butchered a seven-hundred-pound beef on the way up to feed the men. Oh, yes, fell in a hole in the ground like a clodhopper and had a lame back for days. But at least I wasn't one of the many who got tangled up in a hornet's nest and badly stung.

"Had an awful lot of high wind to make the going disagreeable... sometimes had to tie up for half-day stretches on account of it. Lots of rain, too, with underbrush all soaked for camping. Quarter of an inch of ice on the river along the coves and getting the boats off bars continually... made a lot of standing in the cold water.

"Worst was when the rain turned to snow and the mules all mired down and you couldn't tell who had the uglier dispositions, the mules or the men. Then this side of Bird Rapids a tow-line broke four times. And now to-day with the wind the hardest yet... so hard we finally couldn't move the boats... tied up a few miles down the river here and came on up in wagons the rest of the way."

So the dishes were done and now was the time to open the leave of absence.

"It's like Christmas," Linnie said happily.

And Norman, with assumed childish excitement, took the envelop and opened it.

His mouth turned down in a wry grin. "Application disapproved."

But it was not Norman who went pale with disappointment. The ups and downs of the army life were old experiences to him. Linnie could not sense it. Why, she had counted on it day and night. It just had to be.

"Oh, Norman," she wailed. "I made over all my clothes. I trimmed my hats. I sent to Benton for a fashionable veil."

"Well . . . now," he tried to joke her. "The adjutant general just didn't happen to know about that veil."

But she would not joke about it. And she would have shed bitter tears but for the fact that Norman was here, safe and sound, and no longer need she lie, alone and fearful, listening to the scrabbling feet in the walls and the cries of those lost souls, the coyotes.

Chapter XIX

BECAUSE Norman was safe at home again after the long and lonely months, Linnie would not let herself think too much of her disappointment over the anticipated leave of absence.

"Now don't be another Mrs. Lane, all tears and wails," she would say to herself.

But sometimes she could not help breaking into a truly feminine lament.

"With the last boat gone you couldn't stand the long roundabout trip by Helena, anyway." Norman tried to comfort her, not wanting her to know he had applied again for a leave. "All those miles of wagon riding in the bitter cold ... over that narrow rough road up to Fort Benton ... and then you've only got a good start."

"Oh, I could stand it, all right." She would not allow the long hard journey to be a reason for staying contentedly here.

Try as she would she could not bring herself to look upon the quarters with the same fondness she had bestowed upon them when winter was coming the year before. More and more she found herself looking longingly toward the east and down the river. No woman at the post but did the same. The east was relatives and friends, new hats and fresh food. It was the land of music and paintings, books and plays, churches and schools.

The October day on which the mail came in overland from Fort Benton with her *Ladies' Repository* and a copy of the 1868 *Parlor Annual*, it seemed that she never had such desire to see the outside world.

"If you weren't always so *dictated* to," she said in exasperation. "Just an order from some one and there you go on a long dangerous commission. Another order and you do something else just as hard. Then you ask for a leave. 'No...no, we don't choose to let you have it just now.'"

He grinned at her foolish mimicking and said: "You've given a pretty good definition of a soldier."

At that she ran over to the new dictionary on the desk. "Let's see just what Mr. Webster says about you."

She thumbed through the pages, found the word and read to herself, then threw back her head and laughed.

"Listen! *'Soldier: One engaged in military service. A man of military experience and skill. In most termites a kind of wingless individual differing from the workers in its larger size, large head, and long jaws.'*"

He joined in her laughter, and the whole thing cleared the atmosphere, so that, no longer in her blue mood, she jumped up with: "Well, I must get

some dinner for you, you old wingless individual of
large size, large head, and long jaws."

And then came orders when no orders were expected, with winter coming on. October was into its
second week. Like a bolt from the blue Norman
came in to tell her he was ordered to proceed down
to Fort Buford with seven discharged soldiers, there
to pick up fifty others of the Thirty-first Infantry
and proceed with them to Sioux City and Omaha.

Linnie stood wide-eyed at the shocking news, an
iron spider in one hand and a cooking spoon in the
other.

"But the last boat's gone." She uttered it triumphantly as though that ended the matter.

"We'll just have to take the flatboats. 'Orders is
orders.' "

"The flatboats! Why, you said yourself nobody
could go down so late . . ."

"Maybe we can catch up with the *Benton* somewhere along the way before the freeze."

She had been an army wife for over a year, but
still her mind could not spring quickly to these sudden changes. There was no flexibility in it, she realized, nothing but a great desire to get into a pleasant
home and stay there, never to hear an order again.

"You'll have plenty of fuel and food for the winter," Norman went on, "and first thing in the spring
when navigation opens . . . "

He got no further, for she was saying vehemently: "No . . . oh, no. I'm going with you."

"Not in an open boat, you're not."

The sudden vision of the old dingy quarters without Norman was too much to bear: the snow piled up, the long nights, the dull winter days, the fear of Indians, those scratching feet in the walls, the loneliness of the waiting. It was desolation. It was agony. It was not to be borne.

"Yes, I am, Norman. I *am* going. You can't stop me."

If he was surprised at the passion in her voice, usually so mild or merry, he only said sharply: "You don't know what you're saying. There'll be snow and ice ... the river will freeze any day now."

"I don't care. I'm going. I stayed in the summer but I won't stay in the winter. Nothing could hire me to."

"We'll sleep in our clothes."

"*I* can sleep in my clothes."

"We might have to abandon the boats and walk ... no telling how far."

"*I* can walk."

"It's no joke for husky men ... but for a weak woman...."

She slammed the iron spider down on the cook stove with crashing force and threw the spoon after it.

"I'm going ... I *am* ... I *am!* I'll be right there climbing into a boat."

She was so nearly hysterical that he took her

firmly by the shoulders. "You . . . can . . . not . . . go."
Every word was tense with emphasis.

"Oh, you're hateful!" she was half-crying.

He dropped his hands and turned away from her
with distaste.

As he was walking toward the outer door she
called to him shrilly: "I'm going . . . that's settled.
And I never want to see a dirty Indian again . . . or
a fort . . . or army quarters . . . or an officer . . . or a
soldier . . . or a buffalo hide . . . or a rat . . . or a gun
. . . or . . ." as the door was slamming, "or *you*."

Then she ran to the other room and threw herself
on the bed with convulsive sobbing.

When her paroxysm had spent itself, she rose and
washed her face. Then she went about her work
quietly, picking up the old iron spider almost apolo-
getically and getting an extra good dinner so that in
the lavishness of it Norman could see she was
ashamed of her weakness.

She dreaded his coming in. But when he did come
and was hanging up his coat, without preamble he
said gravely: "All right. You don't know what
you're getting into, but if that's the way you're feeling, you better go."

"I can go?"

"If you think you can stand it."

"I can stand it." She was childishly excited. "Oh,
Norman, of *course* I can stand it."

So exuberant were her spirits in the two days following, so constant her animated chatter, that she

paid little attention to his silence on the whole subject.

It was such a short time, those two days in which to get ready, but every hour counted in the coming race before winter set in.

Norman's every moment from morning until late at night was filled with overseeing the repairing of the boats, turning over his ordnance stores, preparing for the trip's supplies. Tired and uncommunicative, he came in late to drop into bed with little or no comment about her going.

Linnie packed and repacked, made last calls on the officers' wives, recklessly gave away her bullberry jelly and her spiced pumpkin-butter.

Mrs. Lane and Mrs. Houghtaling were at swords' points over the soon-to-be vacated quarters and the big mirror. It was going to take the colonel, that Solomon in uniform, to settle the question of the out-ranking couple. The sewing-machine and the dishes and other household effects were packed and ready to be sent out later.

As a last touch of happy preparation Linnie decided to retrim her brown velvet hat with the pretty buff breasts of four woodcocks they had just eaten.

The Day came, a capital letter day, that eleventh of October, if ever there had been one.

They were up at reveille, expecting to start by seven-thirty, but there were two delays. The company commander not having all his papers ready was one. But the other was occasioned by Linnie appearing down at the shore dressed jauntily for the journey in her silk manteau and kid gloves, with her little butter-bowl hat adorned with the late woodcocks' buff breasts and the new veil from Benton flying behind her in the breeze.

Norman took one look at her and made her, protesting, go back and unpack and get into her warmest dress, layers of underwear, her beaver hood and mittens, and his older buffalo coat, while the little woodcock hat was stuffed ignominiously into one of the boxes.

It seemed queer to say good-by to all the old friends down at the boats. How close the ties in such cramped quarters! Too close at times, Linnie remembered. But now that she was leaving, every one's faults suddenly dropped from them like discarded garments.

The colonel's wife had been a mother to her. Always she would carry through life something from that colonel's wife, a fire lighted from the torch of faithfulness to duty which the plump little woman bore aloft so courageously. Mrs. Norris, the captain's wife: why, her worries and fault-finding were only thwarted ambitions for the children. Mrs. Houghtaling: Linnie found she possessed a great warmth of feeling for the woman who had buried part of herself here in that little alkali mound. Even Mrs. Lane! How could one blame a young woman for her tearful longings, who had been brought up in so fine a home?

As for the officers, the Colonel and Captain Norris, their familiar faces, homely and weather-beaten, looked only kind and fatherly now. Lieutenant Houghtaling and Lieutenant Lane, with their own jealousies fading into a background of memories, seemed her close friends.

But it was the children to whom she dreaded to say good-by, leaving them all until the last.

Jimmie Houghtaling kept up a continual tugging at her sleeve. "When you comin' back?" "Will you come 'n' go fishin' some time?"

Effie and Essie were crying a little, their coarse unlovely hair in their eyes and their roughened knuckles digging at sodden faces. Ezra was not crying. Too big a boy for childish tears, he was only swallowing hard with the occasional snorting of a twisting nose.

Remembering the day of the big scare, Linnie pressed his warty hand. Perhaps he remembered it, too, for he pressed back as though in understanding.

At the last Norman sent some one back to the quarters for an extra roll of buffalo hides. Then they were in the two flatboats ready to pull away. Four men were in the open one, Norman and Linnie and three of the men in the one with a small cylindrical shelter made from planks.

"Good-by! Good-by!"

"A safe trip to you!"

"Don't let those old sand-bars get you."

"Look out for the dirty Injuns."

"Give my love to Omaha."

Ezra Norris was running down the rough shore, waving an arm up and down. Linnie waved back, watching that pumping arm through moist eyes until it faded into a confused background of shore, stockade, and fort. And then she could no longer see the shore, the stockade, or the fort. She was going back to civilization.

Chapter XX

THE day was made for the journey. October sunshine flooded the hills and the river valley. The air was clear with the exhilarating uplift of the new fall. Every yellowing leaf on every cottonwood in the timbered bottoms whirled in its own particular dervish dance. Back upon the hills and in the ravines scrubby pines looked on, stolid wall-flower trees, never joining in the dancing. A long V-shaped flock of geese flew over, squawking smugly because they were able to navigate the blue waters of the sky.

"They think they're smart Alecks, Norman," Linnie laughed, "because they can go on and leave the old boats so far behind."

She was too warm and began taking off some of her wraps, untying her beaver hood and pulling off her big fur mittens.

"I'm like an onion," she called out to Norman. "I could peel off six layers and still be warm."

Her happiness over the coming journey gave her a childish feeling of present joy and anticipation for the future. Light-hearted and talkative, knowing nothing of the hardships to come, she did not notice that Norman's mouth never once turned down at the corners over her gay sallies.

For long hours the sailing along out here on the water in the lovely day was as pleasant as any picnic. And then suddenly the other boat, ahead of them, struck a rock in the rapids, tearing a hole in its side. Leaking badly, it was finally pulled off the rock by the men all getting in the water, and there was delay over the repair. But they made progress afterward and at sundown camped at the first of Dauphin's Rapids, where they ate heartily around the campfire. The plain fare tasted so good! Yes, it was just like a nice picnic which would not end for many days.

When they had finished and the men were lighting their pipes, one broke out into a noisy bass singing of

> *In a little rosewood casket*
> *That is resting on the stand*
> *There's a package of old letters*
> *Written by a . . .*

Norman came loping up to the fire with—"Hey . . . plug up that bunghole, you. You'll get a casket from some young Sioux and it won't be rosewood either."

They all turned in early, with a guard at the fire and another one appointed for the latter half of the night.

"See!" Linnie was crowing a bit over the day's accomplishment. Settled in her small tent, warmly wrapped in her buffalo hide for the cool night, she called to Norman. "It isn't going to be one bit hard."

"I only hope not," was his curt response.

But in the night she woke to hear pattering on the tent, and in the morning there was snow on the ground, not a great deal, just a wet dash of it, as though nature were having her little joke, mischievously throwing a few handfuls of it in their faces.

Morning began for them at four o'clock, and they started on at daylight, having considerable trouble in getting over the rapids. In fact, they hit the rocks many times all that day, with every one but Linnie out in the water to push the boats off. At sundown they camped eight miles below Cow Island.

She found herself more tired than at the close of the first day. The continued low sitting posture of her body, the long hours after such early rising had begun to tell on her. The moment she could do so she unfastened her stays, pinning her skirts' bands loosely over them. Oh, dear, and she had always been so proud of her small waist, too. She had little to say to Norman to-night and merely turned in hastily after supper, thankful that the day had come to its close.

It stayed frosty and clear at night, each day seemingly beginning in cloudiness and ending in the afternoon's mild October sunshine. On the fourth day they passed Fort Hawley and camped at dark at the Musselshell, where they found four other soldiers waiting to join them.

Tired and stiff from sitting so long and so low,

still Linnie could laugh. "I just can't bear to pester you, but who said I couldn't come along?"

"All right," Norman agreed soberly. "You're here, aren't you?"

Gradually it came to her that something more than responsibility for the river's journey was making him so taciturn with her. Always before, even in the midst of serious moments, she could bring a grin to his grave face with some humorous sally. But now he was consistently unresponsive. Maybe he was remembering all those unpleasant things she had said. But surely he should know she didn't mean them. The very first time she had a chance she would talk about it with him. At some opportune moment she would say, "I didn't mean a word of it, Norman," and the corners of his mouth would turn down and he'd say, "I guessed as much."

He was taking his turn at guarding from the Indians and wild animals these nights. No one could ever accuse Norman of holding aloof from the men under him. That which they had to do, he was apt to do first.

It was freezing slightly on the fifth day, and Linnie no longer shed any of her onion layers. All day they moved along in the crisp calm weather, but in the afternoon a strong head-wind came up and retarded them. They saw plenty of game, and just as they were ready to camp at sundown on an island, Norman shot a deer, and the fresh meat made their supper a fine one.

Through that entire night the wind blew a hurricane. It kept Linnie awake with its wild ranting so that it seemed she had only dropped off when Norman shook her, telling her it was three-thirty and they must be ready to start at the first streak of dawn. She was cold and wracked by the wind and the lack of sleep. When he brought her a pan of river water for washing as always, she shuddered at its iciness. Before her tent should be struck she unfastened her waist and many skirt bands, pulling off her hard stays, and rolled them up and stuck them in her satchel. So much for being fashionable!

All day the head-wind blew so that the boat appeared to stand motionless against its onslaught. And all day Linnie stayed under the shelter of wooden planks with the supplies of food. By three in the afternoon Norman decided they could do no better than to tie up and have an early supper. One of the men killed a buffalo while the others made camp, so that they had fresh meat again.

The wind died down, and the next day was still and cloudy. The guard made a mistake in time and called every one at one-twenty, excitedly thinking his watch hands were at five minutes past four. Breakfast was eaten at a ghastly hour and then all turned in and went back to sleep until daylight. That day the boats went hard aground again so that they had to light over the bar with the yawl.

Time and again now the boats were to get aground, but never was there more than a short delay. Sometimes they camped on shore with a fire near-by. Sometimes, if there had been an early supper and a bit of travel afterward, they tied under a cut bank and slept on the boats, without fire. Twice they sighted Indians. Once three red men stood stolidly on the bank watching them pass. But the other time a larger group, a half-dozen mounted men appeared, coming through the brush at various points from a ravine. Their galloping along shore, wheeling and turning, added an ominous touch to the incident. Norman gave orders to make a generous but apparently careless display of guns, and nothing more came of the alarm.

And now they arrived at Fort Peck, where they purchased four days' rations. Then they went on through crooked waters where sand-bars were dangerously thick, until nearly dark, when they camped on a sand island, with rain threatening.

But the rain threat lifted, and the new day turned clear and bright but cold.

Norman's yawl went ahead to find the channel, but even though he took the greatest precaution, the day seemed one endless succession of going aground with all hands out in the water to pull the boats off. They sighted the old wreck of the *Amelia Poe,* camping not far below it, and Linnie, swathed in her shapeless clothes without stays, remembering her first sight of it, could only wonder that she was the same fashionable person who had made that long trip alone so blithely.

And now came morning fog, so dense that they could not start until long after sunrise. When they did, they saw four Indians breaking camp not far away, all thinking but not saying how uneasy their rest would have been had they known this.

Some better days followed now, with the wind favorable and the river good, one day starting as the sun rose blood red.

"Blood on the sun ... do you see that, Lieutenant?" a man asked worriedly.

Norman shrugged. "I've seen blood on the sun and blood on the moon, and still I'm alive."

The wind rose to a gale. The river curved now like some drunken roisterer, to the left—to the right—in letter S fashion, so that in the fierceness of the wind's blowing it was hard to make the turns.

Toward night two Indians slipped silently into cover on the right bank, so that Norman chose to make camp on the left and doubled the guard. But nothing came of it and they had a good run all the next day, except for a two-hour delay with Norman's boat fast on a snag. Always before they had succeeded in getting them off in reasonable time, but now there was nothing to do but unload all that baggage, including Linnie's trunk and satchels and many boxes, until Norman in exasperation asked her why she hadn't brought the big mirror.

There had been no human being in sight all these days besides themselves and the few Indians they had glimpsed. But to-day there were more Indians, an entire hunting party with horses packed, moving silently down on the left bank a little after sunrise. Alert for any warring move on their part, Norman scanned the shore constantly, and toward night when they saw a woodchopper's ranch, he gave orders to camp in the shelter of its timber.

The day that followed found the river the best yet, most free from snags and bars, with the current strong and deep, so that they went along rapidly, stopping for supper on a willow point and moving on until after ten under the light of a bright moon.

Linnie had lost her spontaneous joy over the trip but made a pretended showing of it whenever Norman asked her how she was taking it now.

"Don't you worry about me."

It was beginning to take courage and no small amount of acting to say: "I can stand it." But she would never in the world let him see that she was tired and sore and wretched.

In the morning they found they had made camp by accident directly opposite Fort Union. Fort Buford then was only about two hours away, Norman told her in pleased surprise. He had business there and said they might have to remain several days.

Fort Buford? Why, it was the fifteenth day of the river journey, and they were only arriving at Fort Buford. Omaha then was in a far-distant world toward which these tiny boats were making feeble efforts to travel. It was like a bad dream in which one sees a goal afar off that one can not attain because of leaden limbs refusing to go.

She tried to take pains with her appearance in preparation for seeing the army people stationed there. But it was hard to clean up in the little tent. Surprisingly she found herself clumsy, with such stiffness of body and once nimble fingers that when she tried to get into her stays it was a torturing task. In some subtle way, ten years seemed to have been added to her youthfulness. In mental alarm she wondered whether she would have lasting effects from the tedious journey.

Combing her long hair as carefully as she could by the dying breakfast fire while the men were busy getting the boats ready, she cast her eye longingly toward the box containing her feathered hat. But before she could broach the subject to Norman he was calling her to come at once, and she gave up all thought of breezing into the fort in her woodcock feathers.

It was like getting into civilization to arrive at the fort, itself so very far away from civilization. There was quite a good deal of building going on here.

Norman reported immediately and turned over stores and ordnance to the company commander and gave his statement of a whisky investigation. Then he began to make preparations for the fifty or more men who were going on downriver.

As for Linnie, she could have stayed on happily a week, for she began at once to have the gayest kind of visit. There were five officers' wives, and they went through the formality of a little tea in her honor and even planned a dance on the second night. There was something exhilarating about these new contacts when her life for so long had been welded to that of the Camp Cooke people.

"Norman, let me have my trunk up from the boats," she teased him. "It's been so long since I've had any fun. Please let me blossom out in my red silk, won't you? And besides"—thinking to clinch the argument—"dancing will get all the kinks out of both of us."

Norman said grimly there was more to this trip than a social affair, but he gave in and let her have it brought up. The evening turned out to contain so much laughter and gayety for her in the light of attention from the strange officers that in her wine-colored party dress she was the belle of the ball.

Sometimes she saw Norman watching her gravely while she danced by him, and she smiled back at him so that he might know she was all over her childish temper. She thought when next there came the opportunity she would tell him how sorry she was for those wild things she had said, but they were never alone. Quarters were full, and she was bunked with a lieutenant's wife whose husband had been sent to Fort Stevenson temporarily. So she could only show him by her merry manner that she was her old self, not disliking the army life at all.

Norman's remaining day here was a full one of

preparation for the rest of the trip, getting the necessary papers, loading the baggage for all those men, packing rations.

Reluctantly Linnie put away her finery and laid out the heavy ugly old clothes. Oh, why couldn't army life always be as much fun as those past few days had been?

And then in the afternoon there was wild commotion. Guards on horseback were seen coming toward the fort pushing the herd of cattle ahead of them as fast as they could get them to travel. Probably a hundred redskins were pursuing. And then when the men were trying to fight them off another band rode in between the cattle and the fort. Whooping, shaking buffalo robes, and shooting, they threw the cattle into panic so that they turned on the drivers, tearing madly through them, with the Indians in wild pursuit.

Immediately the infantry turned out. Workmen at their building ran for their arms. The commanding officer ordered out a mounted detachment. The two bands of Indians joined to fight while the steers were being driven away by others.

Three men were killed, three wounded. All others came back, having been able to save only a few head out of what had been perhaps two hundred and fifty beef cattle. The same old story. The United States Army was on the defensive. Too few men and guns. And ironically this was the year of the great tribal gatherings, the year of the peace treaties. Father De

Smet had come all the way up from St. Louis to aid the government at Fort Rice. If there had only been more Father De Smets, as well as soldiers and guns!

All this excitement had thrown Linnie back into her old fears of the Indians. Just as she had forgotten it in the light of the officers' ball, now it was here again, and she was afraid to start out.

But Norman said there would be nothing more for a while, there was always a lull after a raid, and besides she knew when she started—didn't she?— some of the things she was facing.

It silenced her, and she was up at daylight on that last morning of October in 1868 and ready to start.

Below them lay the long, twisting, tortuous course of the river. In the immediate future were the November days when the cold would close in upon those dark waters. You have danced your last gay dance for a long time, Linnie Stafford.

All that day the flotilla of flatboats ran on without accident, and the big crowd of men had supper at sundown. Then, because the moon was getting fuller and the river was somewhat lighted, Norman decided they would run all night.

Linnie curled up in the boat shelter by some boxes of hardtack, a buffalo robe under her head and another over her, and went to sleep. The motion of the boat became the natural thing, so that when it stopped and there were many voices, she awakened. It was a snag again for one of the boats, and all were tying up at three o'clock in the morning.

She lay wrapped in the robe, aching and half ill, recalling the luxury of her warm bed up at Camp Cooke. After a time Norman put his head in the shelter's doorway and had a cup of coffee for her, telling her breakfast was under way. How good he was about her physical comfort! If only he would come close to her again in other ways. His gravity lately appeared to be deeper than his mere usual quiet—a thing of the spirit. He seemed very far away from her, as though he were just one of these sixty men and did not belong to her at all.

Chapter XXI

IN the following two days the flotilla made good
progress. Even though they were grounded several times a day, it was a mere matter of some of
the men getting into the water and releasing the
boats. So many hands made light work of delays
such as these.

The second evening they passed a large camp of
Indians. On the third, Norman decided to run all
night to take advantage of the bright lamp of the
moon. They planned their supper for sundown, then
sat around the fire waiting for the moon to rise.

Some one started singing, "We're Tenting To-
night."

Some one else called out: "We had enough of that
a while back." And the song was booed down to
make way for a group of sentimental ones, "Daisy
Dean" and "Old Elm Tree." Norman did not stop
them as he had done to the smaller group. No Indians would be attacking a big party of armed soldiers in close formation. Their deadliest work was
when stragglers were caught abroad, men with mail
or a few woodchoppers.

Wrapped in her warm buffalo coat Linnie sat at
the doorway of her small tent not far from the fire

and, fatigued as she was, joined in the singing, her voice rising clear and high above the masculine ones:

> *Oh, do you remember the Indian tale*
> *Of the maidens who wept by the creek in the vale*
> *For the braves who were slain in Nehawka?*

Apparently no one gave thought to the incongruity of that emotional singing about the very people which the army was out to suppress. It was the melody for which all had a fondness. Any other words would have sufficed:

> *And the little stream fed by their weeping all day*
> *Rose into a river that wended its way*
> *To the sea with the tears from Nehawka.*

By the time the moon had come up like a great silver balloon Linnie was so tired and sleepy that it seemed almost impossible to stagger down to the boat and start out for the long night's travel. But she had that deep pride over having told Norman she could do anything he asked. So she pushed at her tired body as though it were another person whom she was shoving ahead of herself.

It must have been midnight when she awakened because of close voices. One of the men just outside her shelter was saying they were opposite the abandoned Fort Berthold.

She peeped up over her buffalo robe and edged herself closer to the opening. Yes, she could see the outlines of the old palisades and the fort beyond.

Norman, right in front of her, was rowing steadily, looking straight ahead. She wondered whether he was thinking anything about the place, remembering that queer marriage which was no marriage at all.

It drew her thoughts to their status now and to what their future plans might be. Norman was expecting his leave of absence to be sent to Omaha and had said it would be his opportunity to go to Washington to see if he could do anything about a future pension bureau appointment. But what about her? Not once had he mentioned plans for her. In the excitement and preparation of coming, there had been no discussion over anything beyond the journey. To get away from the post had seemed the end and aim of everything for her. That morning when she had lost her temper, had he heard her when she said that ugly "or you"?

If that's the way you're feeling, you'd better go. A thought clutched at her mind with fingers as icy as the waters below her. *You'd better go.* Maybe he hadn't meant merely to go on the trip. Maybe he'd meant—

For a long time she lay there awake, ill with mental worry in addition to her bodily discomfort. Then she dropped into a disturbed sleep. The next she knew they were docking at Fort Stevenson just at reveille.

Norman had to see a Lieutenant Walborn here, so they went at once to his quarters, where they were welcomed hospitably and had breakfast with the couple and their two little boys. Then he and Linnie went to General de Trobriand's quarters to pay their respects. They found him in his new house, after— as he told them—nine months in a dingy temporary building made of logs and mud where the field mice held a dance every night on the canvas ceiling. Now he had a five-roomed house with rooms upstairs for his servants, and he was feeling quite grand.

He was a heavy-set rather noble-faced Frenchman, this cultured Philippe Regis Denis De Keredern De Trobriand, Commanding Officer of Forts Stevenson, Buford, and Totten. The eldest son of one of Napoleon's generals, he had come to make New York his home and when the war broke out had organized the French Regiment there. Now that the war was over he had been selected as one of the officers to be retained in the reorganized army.

Very courteously and kindly he talked with them, questioned Norman at length about the Montana Territory posts, and paid gallant respects to Linnie, compliments which she felt she could not deserve in her rumpled clothing and unbecoming hood.

Back at the Walborn quarters they took leave of the family and thanked them for their hospitality, never knowing, in the way of unseeing humanity, that three weeks later the lieutenant would lie dead, and his wife and little boys must stay by his temporary grave until the first boat could come down the river the following summer.

And then from this garrison forty-one more discharged soldiers joined the boats, so that the flotilla was still larger.

They made a good run the rest of the day, waiting two hours after supper for the moon to come up and then going on until two o'clock, when the rising wind blew them on to a sand-bar where they had to remain until daylight.

Linnie had grown so used to this great crowd of bewhiskered men around her, their winter regalia topped by a mixed collection of extra coats, mufflers, and fur caps with ear-flaps, that day and night they were a part of her consciousness. She herself wore a pair of men's felt boots now, and when she walked she shuffled like a squaw.

Indeed, with every fiber of her being she knew now how a squaw felt. Don't ask questions. Don't think. Do as you're told. Just follow your man.

Life was all physical, getting your aching body into a better posture, giving your tired head some rest and your empty stomach some food. Emotion had no part in your make-up. Away off yonder—somewhere—women were ambitious and jealous, loved pretty clothes and had social aims. How ridiculous! All any one in the world could ever desire was a roof, a bed, a fire, and something to sustain life. Shelter. Rest. Warmth. Food.

Now the wind was a howling gale. And she was the most distressed she had been on an endless trip which had given her countless hours of discomfort.

She tried sitting up with a robe over her head, lay down again, turned and twisted and bit her lips to keep back tears of nervousness and pain.

They passed a shipwrecked mackinaw with no one in sight, made only four miles' progress in so many hours that they tied up for the rest of the day, starting again at sundown with the dying wind and running all night.

It was colder than it ever had been. Ice collected all night on the oars. Norman brought her an extra skin and tucked it about her. "I never want to see another buffalo hide," she had said a hundred years ago, and now a good warm hide was one of the most priceless things in the world.

But though she wrapped herself tightly in the robes, pulling her feet in their felt boots up high under her heavy clothes, she shivered and could not sleep.

All the next day they bucked the cold wind, so that the skin of her face felt as tightly drawn over the bones as a mummy's. Once she felt something wet on her cracked lips and found it was blood. Norman helped her tie another scarf over her mouth, but the moisture of her breath froze it into a piece of woolen glass.

It was like heaven, then, to dock at Fort Rice in the evening, to see Mrs. Duncliff again, her old roommate of the upriver journey, and to stay all night in the comfortable quarters with her. She took off her clothes, bathed in warm water, combed her hair, put mutton tallow on her cracked lips and hands.

There was a great deal to talk over.

"So you're Mrs. Stafford, a lieutenant's lady?"

"Yes."

"Then you did go up there to get married?"

"No."

"Then you went to visit an officer's wife?"

"No."

"You better explain yourself, Miss."

"I didn't know I was going to be married. I just thought . . ."

"You just thought *what*, Miss?"

How foolish any explanation sounded! You couldn't put this queer love affair between Norman and herself into words.

Mrs. Duncliff asked if she remembered the pilot's wife. She had come all the way up the river this summer to visit her husband's grave; though she was touched in the head, the river pilots treated her like a queen.

There was a long delay in getting started from Fort Rice, caused by Norman's having trouble in obtaining rations for so many men. When he had succeeded in doing so it was afternoon. That made the river run very short for the rest of the day, for there was no more night travel. The moon had gone, and the skies were cloud-laden and very dark.

And then the snow came. All night it fell on the improvised camp and all next day on the open boats.

Linnie lived on a white planet made only of snow

and cold or on a black planet of hairy covering and cold. All the days of her life she had only to smell the wild leathery odor of a hide to relive those days when she crouched under buffalo skins, and there was nothing in the world but falling snow and swaying boats. And always the cold. Night and day, on shore or river, in camp or boat, always the cold.

Sometimes she dreamed of warmth, the heat of summer afternoons, the flames in the fireplace at the quarters, wood burning briskly in the sheet-iron cook stove, the red glow of Uncle Henry's coal-burner. But always she woke to that cold which would not abate. Even by the side of the camp-fires, so hot that one side of her was burning, the other side still shivered and could not get warm.

And now, on a night, they camped in eight inches of snow on the level. By the time they started in the morning, the ice in the river was so heavy that they could only float in the current.

All day she wanted to sleep, but Norman would not let her. How could he be so cruel? Sleep was so comforting. Sleep meant dreams. And dreams meant you could go into warm army quarters or lie down on the hot parade grounds and let the sun pour over your body. But Norman was mean and would bend over her, working her arms up and down and scolding her, telling her crossly to stay awake and wave her own arms about.

Often when he was taking his turn at the oars he would swing around to the opening of the shelter and feel the upper part of her face, asking sharply: "Linnie! Are you all right? Can you stand it?"

And Linnie, always remembering that she was responsible for being here, would try to moisten her cracked lips so she could say, not too thickly: "I can stand it."

Then when even the bravest soldier among them, almost frozen, was getting discouraged, like an answer to prayer there came help. After they had left Grand River and the Agency, there ahead of them lay the steamer *Benton*.

There was lusty shouting and curse-encrusted thanks. The flatboats were tied up to shore to be abandoned.

Norman had much to see to now.

"Which piece of baggage do you choose to take?" he was asking Linnie.

How queer! What was the matter with Norman?

"Why, I want *all* my baggage, Norman."

"There's only one trip to the steamer going to be made," he said shortly and turned to the men. "Any volunteers to leave some of your luggage behind and take my wife's?"

Oh, that was cruel of Norman!

"No ... don't do that."

Several were volunteering to throw away some old carpet-bag. Others were trying to add the satchels and the foolish hatboxes to their own filled arms. Two of them tied their satchels around sturdy necks and swung her trunk between them.

It was precarious embarking from the sandy shore and flatboats, but all made it after much effort and some losing of balance and baggage. Even then they found the vessel had only enough fuel to get them downstream a few miles until they could take on wood.

But that relief from biting winds! That feeling of security with a roof above one's head! If people only knew how good and substantial a roof is, Linnie kept thinking. Thank God for roofs. Something over your head to keep out wind and rain and snow. Even the foxes have holes. No one ought to complain . . . ever . . . who has a roof.

There was a room for her now, with a bed, but both were icy cold. Only by covering up with army blankets and buffalo skins could she stand the freezing atmosphere of the cabin.

The *Benton* started downstream. But by the time it had arrived at the timber land and the wood was cut and on board, the ice on the river was very heavy, so that it made but slow progress, and the snow was coming down fast.

For three days they crawled through the snow slowly, like a child working its timid way along a path of thick bushes. The ice increased. The wind grew stronger. The snow enclosed them like the smothering robe of a giant white buffalo.

On this third day since getting on the boat, they passed Fort Sully and tied up later at Old Sully. The storm cleared, and they crept on through the ice, making but little headway but thankful that the falling snow had been left behind and the way ahead was clear.

They passed old Fort Thompson and jubilantly ran into open water free from ice. But so anxious were they to make up time that they carelessly ran aground almost at once, and the men worked nearly all day in the icy water until they were on the way again.

Then those two old enemies, ice and wind, like un-whipped Sioux, came sneaking back for further fighting.

A whole day they were held up on account of a hurricane-like wind, with the ice gathering and getting stronger every hour. On account of the large crowd and the long delays, supplies gave out. There was only hardtack for all.

Linnie was lying much of the time on the bed for sheer warmth of body, so that now Norman occasionally brought her hardtack and hot water. There had been weevils in the ancient biscuits, for they were perforated, but she nibbled on them and drank the water with nauseous loathing.

And now came a day of thickening ice when the captain said there would be no hope of getting away at all unless it was done the first thing next morning.

Every man on board was out to watch the get-away at daylight. But night had completely blocked the river. The *Benton* could not move.

All day, then, every man—crew hand, passenger

or soldier—worked, cutting a channel for the yawl
and laying boards on the ice toward shore.

In late afternoon the task was finished, and the
disembarking began.

Norman sent a detachment of men across first
with orders for shore fires. Then he helped Linnie
down to the yawl. She moved slowly and as awk-
wardly as an old lady in her big felt boots and buffalo coat. She felt stiff who was so supple, bowed
down with years who was so youthful.

A night camp was made on the snow-banked land.
Two men were detailed to set out on foot to try to
locate a chopper's cabin or a ranch, in order to get
teams to haul the baggage to Fort Randall, which
could not be far away.

It was sundown when the men started but sunrise before they came back, reporting they had found
a ranch about eight miles down the river and had
hired two ox-teams.

It took all forenoon to get the baggage off the
boat and loaded on to the sleds. Linnie sat by the
fire waiting, a dull creature without initiative or
emotion. Once she caught a glimpse of her own
mud-stained trunk and crushed hat boxes, the gay
flowered paper wet and torn and the end of a blue
feather trailing along in sodden limpness.

Then the sleds were ready and she could ride sitting on a cross board with the driver, packed in robes
and backed by a wall of trunks and satchels.

Norman and his men and the crew, well over a

hundred, tramped along in the snow the eight miles until they reached Pierre Filicia's ranch, where they camped in the stable, and only Linnie had a narrow improvised bed made on three chairs in the ranch-house.

It was four in the morning when Norman came to awaken her, telling her the baggage was all loaded and they wanted to start at daylight. There was warm drink and food, but even with it before her she could not eat. Only the hot tea satisfied her.

Norman could ride with her to-day in an ox-drawn sled.

All day they jolted down the snowy one-track river road, a man and woman bearing the same name, but strangers, too cold and too fatigued to talk. It was late at night when they arrived at Fort Randall, and so there was to be no merry-making here as at Fort Buford, even if Linnie had felt like it. Easing her weary self on to the bed in an absent lieutenant's quarters, she remembered that Fort Buford dance as something which had happened in another world, before she had turned into this stiff old woman whom she did not know or like.

It was nearly noon next day before the last load of baggage came in. Norman had much to see to, starting the men on their long ride to Sioux City. Then he and Linnie set out on the long trip themselves. This time a place for her was arranged among the baggage in the open wagon-box, for, although there was less snow here, the cold and wind seemed harsher than ever and the wagon-seat was more exposed.

And now it was almost as though her brain ceased to function. Now she knew such bodily fatigue that her few thoughts were not quite sensible. There was nothing in the world but an endless journey, nothing in life but unceasing movement. She was going on and on like the horses in the treadmill whose circling plodding knew no finish.

For fifteen miles they jogged that day to the Yankton Agency and stayed all night. Then Norman called her at daybreak again, while every bone in her body cried out and every muscle sagged in weariness.

All morning they rode behind a plodding team, changed horses after fifteen miles, and went on their jolting way. Even the horses could stop, Linnie thought. Only humans had to keep on forever-and-ever-world-without-end-amen. No, "amen" was the close of the prayer, the finish. And this was only a forever-and-ever-world-without-end. There was no finish.

It was sundown when they got to Bow Horn. They had supper there, changed to four horses, and started out again, arriving at Yankton at ten at night, having traveled sixty miles by wagon.

It was snowing again here, but Norman could find no accommodations, so that when a merchant told him they were welcome to sleep in his general store, he accepted the invitation at once.

The merchant gave them a few directions before

he left them. They could wash up back there. Tin basin and pitcher. The lamp was here. Must be careful of the stove for fire. Fire was a worse enemy than the Injuns here on the frontier.

When they were alone Norman spread papers on the floor and took bolts of red flannel from the shelves to make an improvised mattress for Linnie. She sat on a hard straight chair waiting, numb with fatigue. When it was ready she dropped on to it in all her clothes like a panting wild animal which has loped all day toward its den.

She slept as the dead sleep.

In the morning she tried to tidy herself after the many days with no tidying. How could a clean person bear to do the things she was doing, she asked herself. How could a fastidious gentlewoman stand tangled hair and soiled hands? What lady could ever sleep in her clothes and let her finger-nails get dirty and broken? You never knew how like a squaw you were until something akin to a squaw's life happened to you. Nothing mattered now—soiled clothes or body. Nothing counted but to get to the end of the road, wherever that was.

When they were ready to start out for the day, Norman, with something approaching tenderness, said: "Well ... the last long pull to Sioux City ... and then after that a train. Are you all right? Can you stand it?"

They were only words now without meaning, but from force of habit she said them: "I can stand it."

Chapter XXII

T O-DAY was to be the last wagon trip through the intense cold. Because of difficulty in getting a team and driver, they did not get started until late afternoon. Even then there was another long wait while the wagon was being repaired, then a change of horses after thirty-two miles, so it turned out that they drove all night to make the journey.

It was mid forenoon, then, a dark gray November morning, when they finally got into their room at the Clifton House in Sioux City.

Linnie flung herself on the bed where she lapsed into sleep so deep and long—Nature's own plan for her—that it was night-time when she awakened. She found that Norman had removed her shoes and covered her, but she had slept all those hours in her clothes when it had not been necessary.

Norman had bathed and shaved and was looking so neat and civilized that she arose stiffly and began at once to get her own much abused body into a cleanly state.

The men had all come in safely, he said. He had paid off and discharged part of them and had paid himself, too, by the major, for these past months since July.

"It came to five hundred and seventy-six dollars and twelve cents, and I've decided to be big-hearted and give you the twelve cents."

It was the first flash of his familiar drollness, and she laughed immoderately at the bit of humor there in the lamp-lighted hotel room. It was so good to catch a brief glimpse of his old self.

It seemed good, too, to be able to clean up so thoroughly. But try as she would she could not bring back from its harshness the fair soft skin of her face or seal the ugly cracks in her lips or take the rough redness from her once white hands.

And now only the train-ride to Omaha remained.

All day the train rumbled and jerked, cinders from the engine clattering like buckshot on the windows. The coach was stuffy. Norman struggled to open a window for her, but when he succeeded in doing so, the thick gaseous smoke rolled in and he shut it, so that the closeness was unbearable again. And Linnie, who had thought so recently she never again could be warm enough, was nauseated with the heat and the swaying car.

Norman had lapsed into his former silence, and when he did speak his words had only to do with physical things—something on the snowy landscape, the fact that they were late going through St. Johns, the probability that the men would want their pay that evening but were not going to get it until next day. No heart-warming praise for her fairly gritty conduct on the long journey, or a word of reassurance for the future.

Partly from car illness and partly from nervous tension, she sat stiffly on the red plush seat.

She had on her brown wool dress, her silk manteau, and the velvet hat with its woodcocks' breasts and flowing veil. For the first time since the long trying trip she felt clean and neat and stylish. Appraisingly she glanced sideways at Norman. Clean and freshly shaved, with his hair newly trimmed, he was as fine looking as ever in his uniform. Only the tell-tale weather-pounded skin of the soldier gave him any other appearance than that of a city man.

Now with all those physical hardships of the trip behind her, she gave thought for the first time to the close proximity of Omaha and their plans after arriving. To get away from the post had been her one obsession. Where the journey would take her and how it would end had been immaterial. But here it was, almost finished.

Could they two go to Uncle Henry's? No. Norman would never consent to that. It would be embarrassing for every one. Could she go alone? They were her own people and she wanted to see them. But—did she really want to see Cynthia? Over and over in her troubled mind she asked the questions to which there were no answers.

Norman had told her of no plans beyond those of the paying-off of the men. Not once had he mentioned anything except that looked-for leave of absence to be sent here and the vaguely mentioned desire to go on to Washington. Did he intend her to accompany him there?

The long journey down the river had been all physical, a mere holding on to life, entirely a thing of wanting only food, shelter, warmth. With these vital necessities at hand again, she was back in the realm of the mental and the emotional.

Now that the body was satisfied, the mind and heart craved assurance. From the innermost recesses of both, persistent thoughts and feelings kept coming to the fore. That morning Norman came in and said curtly: "If that's the way you're feeling, you better go." Did it have deeper significance than the taking of the journey? Had he shown thoughtful care of her physical welfare all the way downriver only as any man of his natural gallantry would have shown it to the one woman in a crowd of men? What was this vague thing which had come between them? A journey of hardships should have drawn a husband and wife together, and yet here at her elbow sat Norman who had never been so far away.

Round and round went her thoughts, as actively endless as the trip, which had taken six weeks and three days.

The train was four hours late, so it was well into the evening when they got to Council Bluffs, still later when their stage crossed the river by ferry and they were really in Omaha.

Suddenly Linnie remembered how some one had

told her that *Omaha* meant "above all others on a stream." That was a joke. Why, Omaha was the center of civilization. Only the north country garrisons were above all others on a stream. And the stream was that old Missouri which came from so many hundred miles away, wandering around like a blustering ill-bred buffoon, building up land and tearing it down, so generous and so treacherous, so deep and so shallow, so mild and so mad.

Omaha! It gave her an indescribable sensation. She had been to the end of the world and back again, physically and emotionally. She had left Omaha a gay young girl to whom the unusual possession of a paid passage up the river was the sesame to adventure. She had come back a wife, made so by peculiar circumstances, and she felt no longer gay or young.

The lights all around seemed suddenly very bright and numerous. Lanterns flashing, lamps in windows, even street-lights were all highly brilliant to one over whom only the moon and a camp-fire had shed light for so long.

It was noisy, too, with calls for several hotels and a clatter of dishes from eating-houses. Drummers and soldiers crowded the stage depot and the seats along the side of the hack in which they rode up to the hotel.

The hotel! It gave her a queer feeling of timidity to go into the lighted lobby where so many people were standing. She walked hesitantly, like one who does not quite know his way. She glanced up at Norman to see how it was affecting him, but he looked sure of himself, striding along in his military coat.

There were men around the bar over at one side and several women visible through the door of the ladies' parlor, two or three even in a close knot waiting just this side of the room.

Suddenly she knew she was old-fashioned in her manteau. These women had on long stylish cloaks, full-sleeved and trimmed with wide silk fringe.

While Norman left her to go to the desk she shrank back from the main lighted part of the room. That bone stiffness and body soreness, those chapped lips and rough hands and the drawn tight feeling of her skin alone would have given her a sense of shyness before these women. And now her clothes were not right. She who had once been a belle in this very hostelry had the feeling of not belonging here, of having come from some backwoods region to this gay one of hanging lamps and red plush chairs.

It was just as Norman was returning to her that simultaneously they saw him. Uncle Henry was coming out of the dining-room door and was stopping to speak to a waiter.

Both unconsciously watching, they saw him look their way without interest, hesitate for a moment in wonderment and then, upon full recognition, come toward them.

"Linnie! And Lieutenant Stafford!"

He was noisy about his approach, so that several people turned toward them. His surprise at seeing them, the familiar old bluster, but above all his apparent pleasure, affected Linnie unaccountably. She wanted to put her head upon that expanse of vest held down by great gold links of a chain and cry.

He gave her a loud and whiskery kiss, patted her shoulders, pumped Norman's hand, asked questions loudly and answered them himself.

"Cynthia's here in the ladies' parlor," he beamed. "We've just had the monthly dinner of our newly organized club. I'll get her."

"No ... oh, no," Linnie said in alarm. "Don't bother her."

But one might as well have tried to stop the Missouri's muddy flow as Uncle Henry.

Norman said nothing, merely stood with his steady gray eyes on the double doors of the ladies' parlor.

To Linnie it took on the features of a bad dream, the thought of seeing Cynthia now, without some mental preparation. It was a torturing thing to have Cynthia come and look at her standing here by Norman with chapped skin and cracked lips, dressed in the same old silk manteau she had worn away, her hat trimmed with breasts from some woodcocks they had eaten.

As one pins the mind to a minute and foolish detail in time of mental agony, she kept thinking of those woodcock feathers all the while that Uncle Henry was away and Norman was standing silently with eyes fastened on the doorway through which Cynthia was to come.

And there she was! Uncle Henry brought her out triumphantly, laughed long and loudly that he had not told her who was waiting out here, so that her astonishment, too, was intense.

"Norman! And Linnie!" She had said his name first.

She was in black, a black ribbon entwined through her pale hair and upstanding in a perky bow.

She walked straight to Norman with outstretched hands. And Linnie, her eyes glued to them both as though under some horrible enchantment, saw plainly that old look of fascination and admiration in his face as he drank in Cynthia's white loveliness. Only while a clock ticked off a few seconds somewhere behind them, Linnie came to know he still held Cynthia in his heart.

Then Cynthia dropped Norman's hands and kissed Linnie, with effusive words of welcome, overly sweet, her eyes still rolled toward Norman.

"Of course you're going home with us," Uncle Henry was saying.

"No . . . oh, no." They were both protesting, Linnie vehemently, Norman merely gravely.

"Oh, yes, you are! I put my foot down. No niece of mine can stay in a hotel as long as I have a roof over my head. Don't you say so, Cynthia?"

"I'd admire to have them." Cynthia sparkled.

One unhesitatingly would have picked Linnie for the young woman recently bereft.

Every objection Norman made was met. If he had to pay off the men to-morrow, why, he could come down as early as he wished. The registering didn't matter. Cancel it. They were "put to it" for room these days anyway. Talk of another and larger hotel being built. And a steel railroad bridge would be started now in the spring. Omaha was up-and-coming, all right.

Uncle Henry was noisily wordy about his hospitality, dramatizing the scene, apparently wanting in his showy way to be big about overlooking the fact that Norman once had been his daughter's young man.

There seemed nothing else to do. Neither Norman nor Linnie had consented definitely, but they soon found themselves in the double cutter, the bells jangling and the vehicle lurching first one way and then the other over the deep snow-filled ruts of the streets.

Up at the house they drove into the alley and directly to the barn, turning the bays over to Magnus, who was surprised and pleased to see Miss Linnie.

They all went in the back way, where Olga met them with a finger at her lips but became noisiest of all at the sight of the visitors.

"Not vonce before in my life vas ever I so glad to see von."

Magnus and Olga lived here now in the back

room upstairs, as Aunt Louise had to have so much attention.

There was consultation between Cynthia and her father over breaking the news to Aunt Louise or waiting for morning, with the decision going to the coming day when she would have had her night's rest. If the house were afire, Linnie was thinking, there would be conference over the approach to the telling. Only George Hemming in his innocence had not conformed, blurting out about the runaway marriage.

It was late, and so there was not a great deal of time for prolonged conversation. That which took place was almost whispered. Also, it was largely one-sided, for Uncle Henry wanted them to know how Omaha was progressing, physically, financially, politically. It was a big subject, and he would go into all the astonishing details on the morrow, he promised, with plenty of proof that he himself was the prime instigator of much of the town's improvement. Also, he would explain how many of its new features, luckily and oddly enough, had been located on or near his own property.

Then they all went up the polished stairway, carrying their night lamps.

In the upper hall Cynthia slipped her arm into Linnie's. "Sleep with me, Linnie, and we can visit."

How sweet she smelled—that same *eau de Cologne* odor.

The two men heard her and Linnie's clear answer: "All right, Cynthia, It will be like old times."

Linnie knew she must carry her head high, even though she had become two persons—the friendly cousin and the hurt woman who had seen such an expression on her husband's face as he had never shown to her. She would put on as good a front as Cynthia. In all fairness she would have to admit that Cynthia was unaffectedly carrying out this meeting which could be nothing but embarrassing for all concerned.

So Linnie went to her old room with Cynthia. And Norman said good night and took his lamp and satchel over to the guest-room.

Alone in their room, Cynthia's chatter died away and a strange silence settled upon her. Linnie, too, felt more constrained here than when Uncle Henry had been with them monopolizing the conversation. It was as though unspoken things hovered about the familiar place, some of them ugly and unwelcome.

Cynthia began brushing her hair, its pale waves falling over her shoulders.

Linnie thought: *To-morrow I'm going to work on myself all day with buttermilk on my hands, soft water and vinegar for my hair, scented tallow on my lips.*

Aloud she said: "Cynthia, try as I would, I just couldn't write you how badly I felt . . . about George."

"Let's not talk about it." Cynthia made a gesture with her brush.

She wants to forget it, Linnie thought, just as she always wanted to ignore all unpleasant things.

For a few moments more Cynthia brushed in silence, and when she turned, some of her recent affability had dropped away.

"You never told me what happened . . . where you first saw him again. Even when I asked, you didn't answer that one question."

It had come. There was no use evading it. "I went clear up to Fort Berthold, Cynthia. Instead of sending your passage papers back to him I went up there on them."

"Yes, I knew it. The minute I saw they were gone something told me you were using them. You thought you had me in a corner, didn't you? That I could never say anything to the folks about you using the passage . . . for you knew I'd never told them I had it."

"I really never thought of that, Cynthia. When I started . . . I can scarcely explain it . . . but I didn't know myself for sure that I was going."

"But you had the passage papers all handy in case you'd decide to?"

How terrible it sounded when put into cold sneering words.

"Yes."

"But what did you *do?* Just *throw* yourself at him?"

Oh, if only she had a right to be angry. But it was so nearly true. How could she explain to this

girl—this disloyal person—that queer impelling
loyalty which carried her on? How natural it had
seemed up there that she and Norman were together who were meant to be. But she couldn't put
that thing of the spirit into words.

"You were already married, Cynthia . . . after jilt-
ing Norman . . . and so I don't believe you have the
right to ask."

"Ha!" It was a short laugh and a cutting one.

They were mortifying moments in contrast to the
earlier pleasant part of the evening.

Then, as though she had let slip inadvertently the
garment of her hospitality, Cynthia hurriedly began
telling some trifling items about Virgilla and Victoria. But the harm had been done, and they went
to bed in miserable silence, a great barrier between
them.

Linnie lay stiffly, staring into the night, colder
than she had been when coming down the river with
the men. Of one thing she felt sure. Cynthia wanted
Norman. She had chosen George first, but now she
was free and she wanted Norman. *You can't have
that doll either, Linnie. They're all mine.*

She pictured Norman's face as he caught sight
of Cynthia in the hotel, admiration and fascination
so plainly stamped on it.

Hours after Cynthia was asleep, her pretty face
in soft repose on the pillow, Linnie still stared into
the darkness, her thoughts leaping from one sicken-
ing crag to another, but coming back always to

Norman's old love for Cynthia: *Although the ice separates us, the river runs below. That's like my love for you.* No, you never get over a love like that.

For some reason she thought of the big mirror up at the quarters, could even see herself looking laughingly out from it. The girl who once stood before the mirror had vanished as utterly as the shadowy substance in it.

If only she could be that person again, with this terrible knowledge all unknown, she would never find fault with the army life and its hardships. To be the happy wife of Norman away up there without this new revealment would be all she could ask. Thinking of the post now, strangely enough the alarms and hardships were half-forgotten and she was remembering only the cozy evenings with Norman, the fun at the little parties and the Sunday night sings.

Yes, she had bungled everything by taking that journey up the river. And now she had bungled again by insisting on this one down the river. It was true, then! Only the things which come freely make one happy. You can not go out and demand happiness from life, wresting it away as the Indians steal and plunder. When one takes it forcibly, it vanishes.

She had not been wooed like other girls. There had been no courtship and no betrothal. She had thrown herself at Norman, although she never had the courage to put it so boldly. After her foolish adventure he had gone through that ceremony for her temporary protection. Then he had kept her through the long winter. Of course. She was a woman. She could cook and lie by his side. Naturally she appealed to him more than a Mandan or an Arikara. *Some have families back home, too. You can't blame them.*

All night she stared into the darkness in the agony of her thoughts, dropping into a troubled sleep only near the dawn.

Chapter XXIII

SHE felt wretched after her sleepless night, but Cynthia was bright and talkative this morning, sparkling in the presence of masculinity as always. And now the masculinity was Linnie's own husband.

Breakfast was the same big meal she remembered: fried potatoes, fried corn meal mush, sausage, eggs, hot muffins, and molasses syrup—a prolonged affair over which there was much local information from Uncle Henry, gay remarks from Cynthia, and an occasional insertion from Olga as she passed in and out.

In honor of the company Aunt Louise had come to the table, where she murmured faint echoes to Uncle Henry's booming assertions as she picked around the edge of a fried egg with the dainty pecking of a newly hatched chick.

There was a time when this good food would have looked like a prince's banquet to Linnie, but now she was having almost as hard a time as Aunt Louise to get it down. For that great weight of combined worries lay heavily on her, the ill-timed meeting of them all and its apparent results, the uncertainty of the future, with Norman saying nothing about plans for her or giving a sign of what he wanted her to do.

It was like theatricals up at the post, this sitting around a table taking the various parts in a play. Soon the curtain would be pulled across the ropes, and the stamping and whistling of the soldiers would follow. No, all that was fanciful. This particular play must go on, each in his part. And her own part was the tragic one.

And then, as though in answer to her questioning, Uncle Henry suddenly thought of some one besides himself.

"What are your plans, Lieutenant?" Even then, between bites of sausage and muffins, it sounded more politely conversational than interested.

"I'm looking for approval of a leave of absence application. Rather expect it's here waiting for me. If I get it I'm going to Washington. Have reason to think I can get in the pension bureau in time. Work there will be increasing now as the men grow older."

It set Uncle Henry off. "Pensions! This agitation over pensions! Paying a man for doing his duty. I'd like some one to pension me one of these days for sticking to my business."

"Yes . . . Henry . . . you're sticking to your business," Aunt Louise said in her little-chicken voice.

Linnie felt such a sudden resentment that her throat throbbed in its anger. She thought of that five hundred and sixty-eight dollars and twelve cents pay for Norman's work since the first of July. Pay for camping on the Musselshell, chasing marauders through the hills, tramping through rains, sleeping in snows, caulking boats with his shirt, the long journey down the river with all its mishaps and discomforts. He was so fearless—so faithful—so responsible. There were careless men in the army, and shirkers—but they were a courageous lot. Their small wages couldn't pay for all they had to go through. The money in the mint wasn't enough to recompense the Indian-fighting army.

But they were eating Uncle Henry's food and so she must say nothing.

"The country's already got a two billion dollar debt. Say that over and see if you can sense it. Not millions... *two billions*. I doubt if the country'll ever take on a load like that again once it's settled. And now agitation for pensions. And who'll pay 'em in the long run?" Uncle Henry snapped at a forkful of sausage. "Citizens like me."

While his beard waggled over the masticating, Aunt Louise echoed: "Yes, citizens like me... us."

"We're the ones who'll have to go down in our jeans. Work hard ourselves and then have to pay the other fellow for doing *his* rightful work. If he can't save against his sickness and rainy day... it's his own fault."

The Regulars protecting the western country, fighting off Indian raids, going into far places where there was nothing but loneliness and danger! Sometimes without good equipment, lacking new guns and sufficient ammunition. All so that Uncle Henry could live in peace in the new west and get fat and paunchy and buy Union Pacific shares and bank stock and Omaha property.

She glanced at Norman and knew he must be angry and resentful, too. How she understood him! Oh, nothing ought to come between her and Norman, ever.

But something *had* come between them: his old love for Cynthia. There was no use to pretend otherwise. For a time, while Uncle Henry was talking, she had forgotten. She had been standing up for Norman and the army in her thoughts just as though she belonged to them both. It gave her a poignant moment to recall how matters used to be. It was true then, what Mr. Tennyson had written, that a sorrow's crown of sorrow was remembering happier things. Once she had liked the verses only for their rhythm. Now she knew their deepest meaning.

"What's the matter with the army anyway?" Uncle Henry wanted to go on with his grievance. "Why don't they clean the damn Injuns out and get it over with?"

"Yes, clean out . . ." Almost had Aunt Louise said the word, too. But she stopped at the brink of the chasm and looked around with scared realization of her narrow escape.

"Making such long drawn-out work of it! Holding on to their jobs, I guess. Phil Sheridan's the one with the right idea. Clean 'em all out in the winter.

Trap 'em in winter quarters like animals. He and Custer'll show 'em."

As his voice grew louder, Polly thumped her scabby old legs excitedly up and down in the cage and called out: "Fit to kill."

"They say Custer started out from Camp Supply just the other day with the Seventh Cavalry . . . a lot of new recruits, too. Going to clean up all of his part of the country. Custer'll give the vermin hell."

Aunt Louise and Cynthia jumped at the exploded word. But Linnie did not wince. Too many muleteers and tough old soldiers had been a part of her recent education. But her eyes were on Norman. Custer was a show-off, Norman had said once in a rare moment of criticism. Surely he would say something now.

But Norman appeared intent on his sausage cake and when he spoke it was mild. "There are good Indians and bad ones, just as there are good and bad white people. And there are quite a few of both running around loose, you know. It'll take something more than Custer and his men to bring peace. For one thing, the government might try settling on some one policy and not change it every year."

The long meal came to a close. Norman, anxious to get his mail and pay off the men, went downtown with Uncle Henry. They left directly from the barn, Magnus driving them out of the alley in the cutter, the bays prancing and bells jingling.

The household life went on without visible disturbance, calm waters over turbulent undercurrents. Aunt Louise in a comfortable chair, her little bloodless feet on a warm soapstone, made buttonholes in a wrapper. Cynthia in a black and white print, with a black ribbon tied fetchingly in her pale hair, cleaned the parrot's cage, dusted, talked pleasantly of inconsequentials. It was as though she wanted Linnie not to remember last evening at all. Olga came in sometimes, taking part in the visiting with Linnie, friendlily unaware that she was out of her place. Linnie washed her thick hair and dried it by the big heater, while all the visiting covered her questioning thoughts.

"How are the winters up there, Linnie?"

"Very cold, of course, but it's a dry kind of cold." *Oh, Norman, what shall I do?*

As she had taken things into her own hands last year she ought to take them now. It was just pretense to think you were weak with indecision when once you had been so strong and adventurous. But she did not know what to plan or do. So she continued to live in a vacuum, feeling a numbness of spirit, speaking trivial things to hide those which were immeasurably important.

When the two men came home for the midday dinner Norman had paid off all the men, but he had no mail. Admittedly disappointed, he said he had thought surely his leave of absence would have been awaiting him.

There was another heavy meal. Uncle Henry attacked it as vigorously as though he had not eaten a huge breakfast. And there was another emphatic monologue from him—the qualifications of Grant for his coming administration and the leading part Uncle Henry had played in the local election, more of Omaha's future and the frank confession of his own essential value to the place.

After dinner the two men went back to the office.

That great weight, like a crushing stone, bore down upon Linnie. She had stood the six weeks' journey with every bone in her body aching and every muscle crying out, and because of her youth had sprung out of its resulting weariness with resilience. But she could not stand this mental stress. Every emotion was pulled to the limit of her capacity for feeling. If something did not happen soon to relieve her, she must snap like a taut old fiddle-string.

Victoria and Virgilla sent word by Magnus they would come to call in the evening.

"We'll all make molasses pop-corn balls in the kitchen," Cynthia said gaily, "and end by singing around the piano. It'll be just like old times."

Oh, how could Cynthia chirp about pop-corn balls and old times when George was dead and this thing —whatever it was—had happened.

Toward nightfall the girls changed their dresses. Olga began getting supper. Life was just one continuous meal here, Linnie was thinking. She sat by Aunt Louise in the back parlor with its familiar horsehair sofa and red afghan, the heavy chairs and their antimacassars, and sad Lincoln in his black frame looking down. The early dusk was near at hand.

It was another world entirely than the one in which so recently she had lived. It was a luxurious world where one stayed warm and well-fed and peaceful. When you looked out of the window you saw homes and fences, a church and a schoolhouse. And though you saw the Missouri River, it was not an enemy here to hold you prisoner with its ice. And though you heard harsh sounds out on the hill streets they were not war cries. But in spite of craving all this, of having felt such deep distaste at times for the post, she never would complain again, if only she might be allowed to go back with this crushing weight lifted.

Out in the dining-room Cynthia was placing the flat silver on the long white cloth and the blue castor which Aunt Louise had brought from Massachusetts and which had looked upon every meal in this household.

Olga came in to take the chimney from the flowered hanging lamp over the table and then went back to her cooking.

And now every one could hear the jingle of the cutter bells in the alley, then Uncle Henry's loud voice as he stomped heavily and wanted to know if Norman was here.

He came through the kitchen to the dining-room

door and called in to the womenfolks that he and
Norman must have missed each other, and he would
go right out and tell Magnus not to unhitch.

But there was no need, for Norman even then
was passing the dining-room windows, swinging
along the walk leading from the front of the house.

Uncle Henry came on into the back parlor and
stood warming himself at the burner.

Norman, too, was stomping snow and then coming
on through the kitchen to the dining-room. From
where she sat, in the glass of the big mahogany sideboard, Linnie could see Cynthia leave the table and
slip over to the door, could see her put her hand
on Norman's arm, tilt her smiling face up to him
and say something. Norman put his hand over
Cynthia's.

It was unbearable to see more. So Linnie stood
up hurriedly and made pretense of straightening the
antimacassar at the back of her chair.

Beyond those open double doors her world was
tumbling through space. If it had to be, it had to be
—but she could not watch it fall.

Then, suddenly, Norman was striding into the
room, his big army coat thrown open, the chill of
the wintry day coming in with him.

Linnie's fingers dug into the mesh of the tidy, for
something about him seemed decisive and final. Un-
mistakably he had that air of snapping into military
precision she had learned to know so well. He had
settled it, then—the only thing in life that mattered.

Cynthia, too, was there, a strange look on her face. It was one which Linnie had never seen before, and she could not translate it. Nor was there time to do so.

For Norman was speaking crisply: "Well, I got it. A little surprise, too!" He was snapping a paper across his gloved hand. "Leave of absence disapproved. Orders to proceed at once to Fort Leavenworth."

Linnie could not take her gaze from his face. Queer how he was looking across at her and at no other, his steady gray eyes searching out and holding her own in the gathering shadows of the November afternoon.

" 'Orders is orders.' "

Something was happening. He was crossing the room and coming toward her. He was by her now, and was putting his arm around her, his gloved hand pressing hard on her shoulder. He was drawing her so close to his side she could feel the steel muscles of his body.

All her life the picture was to be etched on her mind: Uncle Henry, big and pompous, melting snow still on his whiskers, his great gold chain across his vest, standing in front of the burner in questioning attitude. Aunt Louise, in her low chair, her plaintive little face with the big ears standing out from it like handles on a cup, looking up startled. Olga, behind them in the dining-room, frozen into a statue of curiosity with one raised arm holding a chimney up to the lamp. Cynthia by the doorway in her mushroom black dress (but a scarlet ribbon in her hair), with that queer baffled look on her face.

Norman was speaking to them. It couldn't be real. But it was. It sounded far off, and like something forever desired but never put into words.

"Uncle Henry ... Aunt Louise ... Cousin Cynthia ... and Olga, you, too ... I want you to know that this little lady is just about the only thing that makes the old army life livable."

He was looking down at her, the corners of his mouth beginning to curve down in their droll grin.

"She doesn't like Indians ... or army quarters ... or army food ... or guns ... or mules ... or buffalo hides ... but luckily she likes *me*. Well, how about it? Another move at once. Are you disappointed?"

This was it. This was her wooing. No matter whether or not Cynthia still fascinated him. Never stop to question it. Never stop to analyze. Grasp happiness quickly before it can flee. This was her courtship and her betrothal. He had said it before Cynthia. He had said it before them all. This was her family wedding.

"Can you stand it?"

Long years stretched ahead filled with Indian alarms and wild animals, dust and blizzards, jealousies and disappointments, endless journeyings, creaking wagons, and bugs and rancid butter. There would be days and nights of anguish and worry and fright. But never mind that. Follow your man. Make him a home with a table-cloth and a cracker box—

"I can stand it. Oh, Norman ... *with you* ... I can always stand it."

It was three-quarters of a century ago that the diary was written, with its innermost thoughts, its current happenings, and its weather. Thoughts and happenings the world over have changed materially, and only the weather is constant in its inconstancy.

The old wooden stockades and forts are gone now, except as an occasional one has been restored for the edification of tourists who buy colored post-cards therein and send them home by air faster than any wild goose ever flew. Scores of bridges cross the Missouri where never a bridge then stood.

No more do the passenger boats ply up and down the old river. And no one ever sings the sad sweet song about the maidens who wept by the creek in the vale for the braves who were slain in Nehawka.

Linnie Colsworth Stafford followed her man from post to post, in cold climes and warm, all the years of his activity until his retirement, packing and un-packing her silver, china, books, and tidies, and an old picture of a pretty cousin eternally smiling from a white carved frame.

The lieutenant's lady lived to be very old, so old that she had seen her son and two of her grandsons in the United States Army and a toddling great-grandson marching and counter-marching with wooden gun.

They say that on the day of her death, after long hours of stupid silence, old Mrs. Stafford roused suddenly and struggled to sit up in bed, saying clearly: "What're those sounds?"

The nurse ran capable fingers over the cold old forehead. "Why . . . what are they like?"

"Kind of like bugles."

And maybe they were. Maybe they were the echoes of bugles from a hundred bleak American camps and outposts and frontier forts—from San Juan Hill and Belleau Wood and the Island of Luzon.